Praise for *The Mother Who Stayed*

"No book could be more beautifully formed or more deeply satisfy-
ing than *The Mother Who Sta*

ing and correcting each other,

accuracy, Laura Furman has t

lated, lacking, and real—in ric

—Joan Silber, author of *The*

"In these powerful and exquisite stories, Laura Furman pieces
words together like shapes in a gorgeous crazy quilt. Each character
and setting is so vividly realized that by the last page I knew these
women and could imagine finding their homes without a map. I
loved this book and, like the best fiction, it has changed me."
—Julie Metz, author of the *New York Times*

"I love these stories.
moving, and making
life. I don't ask for any

f**P**

ALSO BY LAURA FURMAN

Fiction
The Glass House
The Shadow Line
Watch Time Fly
Tuxedo Park
Drinking with the Cook

Memoir
Ordinary Paradise

THE
MOTHER
WHO
STAYED

Stories

LAURA FURMAN

FREE PRESS

New York London Toronto Sydney

*f*P
FREE PRESS
A Division of Simon & Schuster, Inc.
1230 Avenue of the Americas
New York, NY 10020

First Free Press trade paperback edition February 2011

FREE PRESS and colophon are trademarks of Simon & Schuster, Inc.

For information about special discounts for bulk purchases, please contact Simon & Schuster Special Sales at 1-866-506-1949 or business@simonandschuster.com.

The Simon & Schuster Speakers Bureau can bring authors to your live event. For more information or to book an event contact the Simon & Schuster Speakers Bureau at 1-866-248-3049 or visit our website at www.simonspeakers.com.

Credits for previously published stories appear on page 197–198.

Designed by Carla Jayne Jones

Manufactured in the United States of America

1   3   5   7   9   10   8   6   4   2

Library of Congress Cataloging-in-Publication Data
Furman, Laura.
The mother who stayed: stories / Laura Furman.
p. cm.
I. Title.
PS3556.U745M68 2010
813'.54—dc22   2010012906

ISBN 978-1-4391-9465-2
ISBN 978-1-4391-9466-9 (ebook)

For Joel Warren Barna and Solomon Barna, with all my love

The author wishes to thank the American Academy in Rome, the National Endowment for the Arts, The Persistence Foundation, the Department of English and the Susan Taylor McDaniel Professorship in Creative Writing at the University of Texas at Austin, and the Corporation of Yaddo for the meaningful support given during the writing of the present collection.

—LF

Contents

FIRST TRIO *1*
The Eye *3*
The Hospital Room *21*
The Thief *30*

SECOND TRIO *45*
A Thousand Words *47*
Here It Was, November *61*
The Blue Wall *84*

THIRD TRIO *105*
The Blue Birds Come Today *107*
Plum Creek *119*
The Mother Who Stayed *126*

First Trio

The Eye

The Hospital Room

The Thief

The Eye

The grape arbor was a square open to the sky with tangled vines for walls. There was no breeze, no sound but the sun crackling in midday fullness and the hum of bees at work. An hour had to pass before the girls were allowed to swim, so they lay in the grape arbor, waiting. When it was very hot, Rachel Cantor's mother had told her, the best thing was to lie still and let the heat leave your body, but Rachel had the beginning of a summer cold and to her ears the bees in the viney walls sounded dangerous. She asked, "Where's Mom?"

"Don't bother her," Betsey Ziegelman said. "She's with my mom."

"They're talking," Katie Ziegelman said.

"They're always talking," said Leah, Rachel's older sister.

Much later, when they were in their twenties, the Ziegelman sisters became famous for their politics. Betsey went underground and never emerged, and Katie wrote a book about her missing sister. Leah Cantor became a criminal defense attorney, though she had nothing to do with her childhood friend.

The vines moved the tiniest bit from side to side.

Rachel stood up; the sky shifted in a sickening way, and she touched her head.

"What's wrong now?" To Leah, any complaint of her sister's was a trick to get attention.

Rachel told her feet to move; through the prickly blades of grass, she felt the earth. With each step she listened for Leah or the Ziegelman girls to call her back.

In between the arbor and the white house with dark shutters Rachel passed the garage with bays for six cars. Harris Ziegelman, Betsey and Katie's father, kept his 1936 cream-colored Buick convertible polished and in perfect shape. Once in a while he'd invite all the children for a ride, allowing them to fill the rumble seat. When they started down the long driveway, the children were free to stick their heads and arms outside the car.

Eva Cantor was on the patio with Helen Ziegelman, saying, "Everything turns out okay in the end. It's awful now, but to tell the truth—"

She spotted Rachel standing with one foot on the slate patio and one on the lawn.

"Sweetie," she said. "I thought you girls were resting after lunch."

"My head hurts."

Eva opened her arms and said, "Poor you. Poor Rachel's getting a summer cold."

"They're the worst," Mrs. Ziegelman said.

Rachel lay down next to her mother on the chaise longue, closed her eyes, and moved her leg so that her foot dangled over her baby sister Emma, who slept in a basket nearby.

"Don't squirm." Eva pulled Rachel's leg in and held Rachel against her, cupping her forehead.

"Poor you," she said, not to Rachel.

"You mean poor Scotty," Helen said. "At least I can afford . . . But—what a mess."

"I feel terrible for your girls," Eva said. "But they're strong."

"There's not a thing I can do about it except—nothing."

"This too shall pass," Eva said. "You don't know what the future will bring."

When her mother spoke that way, which she did often, Rachel was reassured in her belief that the future was a place—like the general store where they went for the Sunday paper and five pennies' worth of candy—only no one knew how to get there.

"You'd think he'd think," Eva said. "With so much at stake. Your life together. The children . . ."

Mrs. Ziegelman laughed.

"Eva, you're a naïf."

Rachel fell asleep to the sound of their voices, and Helen picked up her camera. Eva's lipsticked mouth was a dark shape against her tanned skin. Her hair fell in waves, one point of her white shirt collar hidden by the sweater resting over her shoulders. Her sunglasses reflected Helen as she held the camera. When Eva was long dead and she herself very old, Helen told Rachel she'd never known a woman so happy in her life as Eva Cantor.

Every year, when summer came, the Cantors moved to the country; so did the Scotts and the Ziegelmans. During the week, Sam Cantor and Ellison Scott worked in the city, and they arrived on Friday nights at twilight, their seersucker suits rumpled, their breath perfumed by the gin-and-tonics they'd consumed on the train.

Harris Ziegelman didn't work in the city in the summer; he had business in the country, the business of being rich, Sam Cantor said. When Rachel asked her father about the Ziegelman money, Sam said that they wouldn't talk about it anymore.

Summers, the Cantors lived in a brown-shingle farmhouse with a blueberry field on one side and a brook on the other. Their land extended into the woods to a crooked old fencepost; it was a patch compared to their neighbor's dairy farm or the Ziegelman land that went on for miles.

The Scotts had a cabin by a lake, with a bedroom for the parents and a loft where the children slept. The one time they came to the country for Thanksgiving, the Scotts stayed with the Cantors because their place had no insulation. "It's like camping," Mr. Scott said, "like pioneering," and it did remind Rachel of a diorama she'd made in a shoebox, of a house in Colonial America.

The Ziegelman house with its many rooms was the center of social life; the dining room was big enough for all of them at Thanksgiving, and there was a living room no one went into all summer. Once night came, the grown-ups gravitated to the den with its stuffed bookshelves and knotty pine paneling, and the chintz-covered furniture with its familiar sags and lumps. On warm nights the grown-ups spilled onto the patio, filling the world with their drinks and cigarettes, their eternal talking and laughing.

The Ziegelmans' cook came with them to the country, a stout, white-haired woman named Jocelyn who always seemed to be on duty, preparing the next meal, providing cookies and glasses of juice when the children trudged up the hill from the pond, wrapped in towels, their lips blue. She warned them not to drip on the kitchen floor. "Back outside! Strip off your suits," she'd tell them, pointing to the clothesline by the door.

This particular summer, each family had a new baby. The Cantor baby was Emma; Lily was the new Ziegelman. The Scott baby was redheaded like his mother's mother, like his two brothers. Baby Lily had a young nurse, and often when the children came into the Ziegelman kitchen after swimming, the baby was on her nurse's lap, and the nurse would say, "We're having our delicious cup of tea."

A few times each summer, all the children had a sleepover. In someone else's house everything was different, even the night sounds. That's how possessive the children felt in the country. Their birds. Their frogs.

On the winding road to the train station, Leah held the baby in her arms in the front seat while Eva drove. Rachel stretched out on the backseat of the Studebaker; the clouds passed in a blur between the lacy crowns of the trees. Eva was worried about being late, so they arrived before other cars with mothers and children took the best places in the parking lot. It was their custom at the station for Leah and Rachel to parade up and down the platform waiting for the train to make its monstrous entrance. This time Leah went alone, and Eva held the baby in her arms and watched Leah while Rachel stayed in the car. Eventually, the parking lot was filled, the train came roaring and clattering, and the men crossed the gravel between the tracks to the children and women on the platform.

Her father's voice was like velvet as he leaned his head into the car, saying, "Where's Rachel?" Before she could sit up, he was taking the baby from Eva and saying, "Here she is. Here she is, sweet baby Emma." He swung the baby up to the sky and she called out in her bird voice.

"Oh, Sam," Eva said.

When Rachel sat up to make room for Leah in the backseat, her parents were in each other's arms, the baby squashed between them. Rachel noticed that her parents were handsome only when they were together; apart, they were collections of familiar flesh, a wave of dark hair, brown eyes looking her way.

"Mom, sit with me," Rachel said.

"I'm up front with Emma and your father," Eva said. "Leah's with you."

"She'd better not make me sick," Leah said. She moved to the window, as far from Rachel as she could. "Tomorrow's the Ziegelman party."

"Fancy soirée for fancy people," Sam said.

"The Ziegelmans aren't fancy and neither are we," Eva said. "Don't start."

"Sorry," Sam said, and when they were clear of the station he began whistling "Buttercup" from his favorite Gilbert and Sullivan.

They passed horse farms with white fences and the Black Angus farm, drove up the mountain through the darkening woods until they emerged at the broad cornfields and the last two dairy farms before home. The Holsteins, Sam remarked, were as well dressed as ever.

"You can never go wrong with black and white," Eva said. "Long weekend, Sam. We have you for three whole days."

"I'll do the garage tomorrow morning."

"It's up to you. It's your holiday."

In the garage, once a small barn, a horse stall housed wooden skis from Sam's medical school days in Vienna before the war. Leather harnesses rotted on the dirt floor. The workbench was covered with cans of screws and nails, rusty saws, frozen pliers, and files as long as their arms that the girls weren't supposed to touch. Clamped to the bench was a grindstone Rachel cranked until the handle spun out of her hand. Rachel dreaded the day, never to come, when all the old things would be gone, their car resting on one side, and on the other a neat workshop, the goal Sam and Eva often spoke of on the way home from the train.

For dinner there was fried chicken Eva had prepared that morning, cucumbers from the garden, and corn from a farm stand on the way to the train. It was Rachel's job to accompany her father out to the front porch to shuck the corn; they spread newspaper to catch the silk and husks. This evening Leah went with Sam, and Rachel stayed on the couch in the parlor next to the wooden radio, eyes closed, listening to her mother filling the corn pot with water and opening the cabinet for the salt, striking a wooden match. The gas burner popped awake. Eva filled the smallest pot to heat Emma's bottle; Rachel heard her telling the baby so. Next thing, her own name was being called. They waited for her at the kitchen table. The yellow ears of corn were steaming, the fried chicken was piled high, and the cucumbers and dill shone like ice in the sun.

"Summer's the fast one," Sam was saying. "Remember Memorial Day? You girls thought school would never end."

"The twenty-ninth of May," Leah said. "We moved to the country the same day Edmund Hillary climbed Mount Everest. It was a Friday."

Eva said, "The way you keep track of things. Please pass the corn, Rachel."

"It's already July third," Sam said. "Tomorrow's the Fourth and we go to the Ziegelmans'. Before we know it, it'll be Mom's birthday and then Leah's, then Labor Day, back to school, then Thanksgiving at the Ziegelmans', then—"

"Sam!" Eva said. "We just got here."

"That's what it's like when you live in a routine," Sam said. "One thing follows another as night the day. May I have some of that corn, Rachel?"

She pushed the heavy platter toward him.

"None for you?"

"She's still under the weather, aren't you, sweetie?" Eva said. "Can you eat a bite? No? Maybe you'd like to be excused."

Rachel's bed was right above the kitchen; the open grate in the floor allowed her to hear everything that went on below. In the winter, heat rose to the girls' bedroom from the kitchen, and Leah complained that Rachel's side was warmer than hers. Clothes off, pajamas on, Rachel shivered between the cold sheets, listening to silverware tapping the dishes, glasses thumping as they were set back on the table.

Leah asked to be excused. She got a jar from under the sink for catching fireflies, and Eva said what a shame it was that Rachel couldn't go too.

"What's wrong with her exactly?" Sam asked.

"A summer cold."

"Shall I—"

"If she's still feeling low tomorrow," Eva said, "you can take over. Let's see how she does with a good night's sleep."

The screen door slammed behind Leah.

Sam said, "Scotty asked me to lunch yesterday. At that fish

joint near his office. He's pretty down. He figures he doesn't stand a chance."

"Three boys don't give him a greater chance than—"

"It's no use judging," Sam said.

"Hard not to—"

"When it's your friends. But they're all our friends. We shouldn't forget." .

In the morning—the Fourth of July, the day of the town parade and the Ziegelman party—Eva's hand rested on Rachel's forehead.

"I'm getting the thermometer," she said. "You're still warm."

Rachel knew that she had a fever; her skin prickled where the sheet touched.

"Move downstairs to my room, baby. Then I don't have to keep going up and down. Everyone's getting ready for the parade."

In her bedroom, Eva rearranged the sheets, blankets, and pillows for Rachel, then went looking for the thermometer, which Rachel dreaded and Eva must have too, for if she found the thermometer, she'd be unable to find the Vaseline, and without that thick unguent, the thermometer was useless.

Her parents' bed smelled of something sweet, and something sharp and grown-up. Through one window, the hedge of bee balm was just visible. Hummingbirds were ravishing the spiky red flowers. The opposite window gave out to the porch where Sam and Eva and the baby sat in the evenings while Leah and Rachel caught fireflies on the front lawn.

Straight ahead, the open window revealed the maple, taller than the house and much older; its leaves were making complicated music in the air. Sam said that the tree had been a baby when General Washington stayed in his winter headquarters not very far away in Morristown. Perhaps he'd ridden his horse down their road and saw the tree on the rise, a sapling then. Not every little thing a man did, even a man as famous as George Washington, was recorded.

And even if General Washington never rode past or noticed the maple, the fact that he was alive at the same time as the tree, and in Morristown, made the tree a part of history, which meant the past, everyone's past.

One day, Rachel intended to climb the maple. When she finally stood at the top, she'd see the farm next door, the Ziegelmans' house, the Scotts' cabin, all the way back to the city. From the branches at the very top, she'd be able to see what was waiting for everyone she knew.

Eva reappeared, her face set in its worried look.

"Do you know where that thermometer went? It isn't next to your bed or in the bathroom. I looked on top of the radio, on the mantel, and it's nowhere to be found."

She reached across the bed to touch Rachel's forehead and the girl rolled out of the way.

"Oh, honey, I know you don't want to miss the parade but—"

Sam was standing at the door, his tweed cap on.

"Let her come. If she feels bad she can sleep in the car. Rachel hasn't missed a Fourth of July parade in her life."

"Feel her forehead, Sam."

"Rachel wants to come," he said. "How sick could she be?"

Eva looked from Sam to Rachel and shrugged.

"Well, it's not deepest Africa."

"Exactly," he said. "Dress her fast so we get a good place."

Two riders on horseback started the parade, each holding a flagpole and a flag, one of the state of New Jersey, the other the Stars and Stripes. One horse was a dappled gray like a cloudy sky. Memorial Day was a cemetery holiday; the Fourth of July was for cheering.

The Scotts were gathered across the street from the Cantors, and the boys were making faces, trying to get Rachel and Leah to laugh. The Scott boys, all three, became as prosperous as their father never was, and one August met in Colorado to climb a mountain. A snowstorm came up and it was two days before the Scott brothers were found. The boys saluted as the old soldiers marched by in Civil War and Revolutionary War uniforms and the tight collarless jackets of World War I. Then came the GIs and the marines. In the last war, Sam Cantor and Ellison Scott were soldiers together in Italy; Harris Ziegelman was in the navy in California.

Sometimes Mr. Ziegelman drove the girls and Mrs. Ziegelman to the parade in the Buick convertible, but not this year.

Across the street, the Scott parents stood side by side. Georgia Scott was from the South, and she was a beauty. The Scott boys called her *Mother,* and fetched her a drink, her pocketbook, her wrap on a cool summer night. Mrs. Scott was wearing a black straw hat with a wide brim that framed her face, and a sleeveless black dress with a tiny waist and big skirt. Circular white buttons climbed the dress from hem to bust. On her feet she wore little white shoes that laced around her ankles.

"When you're clever and have taste," Eva said, "you don't need money."

The Elks and the Masons came next, the hospital volunteers, the Red Cross, and at the end the kids joined the parade all the way down Main Street until it became the road out of town. Leah ran off with the Scott boys. The Scotts crossed the street to join the Cantors, Mr. Scott carrying their new baby in his arms.

Mrs. Scott kissed Sam and Eva. She inspected Baby Emma, laying her red-nailed finger on the tiny nose.

"What a darling girl," she said. "I'm doomed to be surrounded by men. Boys."

"Your boys are adorable," Eva said. She was wearing her new brown sundress with white piping and flowers along the hem, white sandals and beads; she'd bought the dress on sale the previous summer before she'd become too big with Emma. "We women are fickle creatures, Georgia. We want what we haven't got."

"Never say die," Mr. Scott said. "Four's a charm."

Mrs. Scott groaned.

"Rachel," she said. "Why aren't you with the other children?"

"Rachel's under the weather today," Sam said.

"It's the biggest party of the summer!" Mrs. Scott said. "Pull yourself together, little girl."

"We love the Ziegelman party," Eva said.

"We love the Ziegelman everything," said Mr. Scott. He buried his face in his son's bare stomach and made a farting noise that tickled the baby no end.

The Ziegelmans invited everyone to their Fourth of July party: the family that lived at the end of the driveway and ran the Ziegelman farm, shopkeepers from town, the doctor and the vet, families from neighboring farms, the summer and weekend crowd and their guests, everyone was invited and mostly everyone came. That year, the Cantors were early enough to get a parking spot not far from the house. By the end of the day, cars and trucks would be strung up and down the driveway and along both sides of the road.

Helen Ziegelman was standing at the front door, greeting her guests. She wore a white blouse with a round collar and puffed sleeves, and black toreador pants. Her necklace was deep red and her earrings matched. The jewels twinkled in the sun.

"Dotted swiss!" Eva said. "Wonderful fabric."

"You look pretty as a picture," Sam said, kissing Helen, who smiled and told Sam that the bar was set up on the stone patio. Leah ran off to find the Ziegelman girls and the Scott boys. Rachel's fever made her too slow to keep up so she stayed where she was.

"Things are a little different this year," Mrs. Ziegelman said.

Usually on July Fourth, the tables were handy to the kitchen. On that Fourth only, the food was on picnic tables that edged the pond all the way down the hill. Swimmers could change in the bathhouse, and there were plenty of blankets and towels for the children to sit on and for the mothers and babies.

Sam said he was going to find a drink, and Mrs. Ziegelman and

Eva walked up the path to the house. Rachel watched them, trying to decide where she wanted to be.

Mrs. Scott appeared in her black dress and hat; she stood holding her baby in her arms while Scotty and the boys scattered.

"There you are."

Harris Ziegelman stood next to her.

"Darling Georgia," he said.

She nodded down at Rachel.

"Little pitchers," she said.

"Hey. Why aren't you with the other kids?" he asked.

Rachel shrugged her shoulders.

"Go on," he said. "Go to your mother."

"Harris," Mrs. Scott said, "that's not—"

Without looking back, Rachel walked to the house and went in through the front door, pausing in the foyer at the photographs of the old people who'd first come to America and started the Ziegelman family. She could see Harris Ziegelman's eyebrows on the men with their hats and shawls.

"I barely squeezed into these pants," Mrs. Ziegelman was saying when Rachel went into the kitchen.

"It takes a little time," Eva said. "You've always had a good figure."

"Takes you a little time. Takes me—"

"When do you want the salads out?" Jocelyn asked.

The kitchen table was covered with platters of meat and bowls of all the salads—tuna, chicken, coleslaw, potato, beet, carrot. On top of the egg salad, Jocelyn had arranged slivered almonds. Sam was allergic to nuts. There were no nuts in the Cantor house, ever. Rachel looked at Eva, wanting her to notice their deadly enemy.

The kitchen windows were wide open, overlooking the lawn that reached down to the pond. Family groups were heading down the slope, fathers carrying babies, mothers rolling strollers and leaning their weight backward against the descent, children looping around their parents and other families, chasing one another to the edge of the water. Boys from neighboring farms and from town tossed a ball over the crowd, back and forth, until a father yelled at them to cut it out, they were going to hit someone.

"It's past noon. Everyone's hungry. We might as well serve it all," Helen said. "There's going to be a game later. Harris mowed a field and made a real baseball diamond. It's his surprise for the Scott boys."

"They'll be so impressed," Eva said.

"He wants the fireworks out there this year. After the game. In the outfield."

One of the workers in Mr. Ziegelman's factory in the city had been with the circus before the war, and he knew how to handle fireworks.

"How would you like to give Jocelyn a hand with the food?" Her mother was smiling down at Rachel.

"Is she well enough, Eva?" Mrs. Ziegelman asked.

"Let the girl help," said Jocelyn. "These girls. Start with the Jell-O. Be sure to set it at the far end of the table in the shade. Near the ice and the drinks. In the shade, Rachel."

Jocelyn went to the big refrigerator and slid out a metal tray.

Mrs. Ziegelman said, "Those bowls would look better on the blue tray."

"The girl can carry it down the hill on a kitchen tray," Jocelyn said. "She'll come back for the other."

The bright orange Jell-O cubes rested in glass bowls. One grape was suspended in each square.

Rachel picked up the cold metal tray, and her forearms and wrists stiffened under its weight. The glass bowls shifted uneasily.

Helen Ziegelman opened the kitchen door.

"Careful on the steps," she said.

Rachel passed families standing, talking, surveying the crowd around the pond. The cubes of Jell-O shivered with every step she took. All her life Rachel had been swimming there, but the umbrellas, striped in red, white, and blue, and the many tables made the pond a stranger. One minute the surface of the cold water reflected the sky and clouds like mountains, the next it was rippled and the sky darkened over.

"Rain's coming," an old man's crackling voice announced.

Rachel turned to see who had spoken, and her movement hoisted the tray forward and then up. Rachel stumbled as she tried to catch the tray, and the bowls of Jell-O launched into the air. She fell forward, too. The treacherous hill was strewn with upended bowls and cubes of Jell-O. Rachel's fists, closed as if they still held the tray, were scraped and stained with grass.

"You were in an awful big hurry for such a little girl," said the same voice that had predicted rain, and Rachel started to cry.

Leah appeared with the Ziegelman girls and the Scott boys. They circled Rachel, blocking her view of the adults around them. She heard a voice calling, "Stay back! Stay back! You'll get cut!" Betsey and Katie poked the Jell-O with their bare toes, then Leah and the boys picked up the orange cubes, now covered with grass and dirt, and launched them at the kitchen tray, so engrossed in seeing how much they could pile up and who got to carry the tray that they forgot Rachel. They started up the hill and she trudged behind them, looking down at her feet and up at the house; by the time Rachel reached the top, the other children were in the kitchen. She listened through the screen door to them talking all at once. "Where'd Rachel go?" Jocelyn asked, and Rachel ran back down the hill.

The raucousness of midday was passing into the quiet of late afternoon. There were only a few swimmers in the water as Rachel wandered through the groups seated at the tables around the pond, recognizing some and others not, feeling like a cloud separated from its sky.

She heard the rumble of low voices and followed the sound around to the back of the bathhouse. Her father and Mr. Ziegelman were sitting in aluminum lounge chairs. Their damp hair was slicked back, and they were smoking cigarettes, their bathing suits on the ground near them and their plates of food, risking ants. Drink holders made of bright-colored rubber-coated metal, seen for the first time that summer, were staked in the lawn; each held a glass of pale liquid. Mr. Ziegelman stood up suddenly, knocking his drink holder. Rachel watched it sway back and forth, the cubes of ice in Mr. Ziegelman's drink bobbing as the drink holder swayed, waiting for the drink to spill.

"What the hell are you doing here?"

For the second time that day, Harris Ziegelman looked down at Rachel, and that was the way she recalled him for the rest of her life; he died when Rachel was almost old herself.

Sam threw his cigarette into the grass, and he moved toward Rachel.

"No need, Harris," he said.

"What's that kid doing here?"

Instead of words, tears came. Sam knelt down and rested his hand on Rachel's forehead.

"Let's go home, honey," he said.

In the time it took Sam and Rachel to climb the hill, the sky went from gray with fat clouds to black as night. A storm was coming. Anyone could see that. By the time the Cantors reached their car, a wind came up—"Oh, no," Eva said—and whipped the trees from side to side. They'd traveled no farther than the end of the Ziegelmans' driveway when the Studebaker lurched to a stop. Sam opened his door and sidestepped, hunched, to the side of the road. Cold needles of rain struck inside the car and the baby began to cry.

"Sam!" Eva called.

Leah opened the back door and jumped out, Eva calling, "Don't!" Leah was soon back inside, shivering with the cold.

"He's being sick," she reported.

"Is he all right?"

"How should I know?"

"Here, take the baby while I go to your father," Eva said, but before that could be accomplished, Sam was leaning into the car.

"Eva," he said, "you'd better take over."

They set out again, Eva driving at half the speed Sam would have, not because of the wind vaulting twigs, leaves, even branches into the air, but by her nature.

"It must have been something you ate," Eva said.

"There were almonds on the egg salad," Rachel said.

"Walnuts on the potato salad," said Leah.

"Why didn't you girls *say* so?"

"I tried," Rachel said. Now it seemed to her that she'd gone to the pond to warn her father.

Sam was twisted in the passenger seat, his forehead pressed to the cool glass. He rolled down his window a crack and raised his head to sniff the wet air.

At the crossroads, halfway home, the stop signs were swaying back and forth, dancing for the Cantors, who stared until the closest one started to fall toward the car. Sam shouted, "Gun it!" and the car lurched forward. Eva was maneuvering the car up the sodden driveway when the storm's noise quietened.

"The eye of the storm," Sam announced. "When it passes, the storm'll start again. Wind from the opposite direction."

The baby cried out, and Sam picked her up and started for the house. Leah and Rachel imitated Eva, who was taking off her white sandals, then they ran, shoes in their hands, to the house. When they were all in the kitchen, Sam said, "Too bad I didn't get to the garage, Eva. We could have put the car inside."

The storm took up again, just as Sam had predicted, fiercer now than before. The power was out. Later, they ate leftovers by candlelight, except for Sam, who didn't eat anything but didn't want to leave them. He shivered in his seat at the head of the table, though he was wrapped in a blanket. Eva sent the girls up to bed.

In the middle of the night the world tore itself apart, and the house shook mightily. Glass rattled in the windowpanes, doors shuddered in their casements. Lightning brightened the rooms and thunder boomed. There was no difference between sound and light. Then came the noise of a heart being ripped from its chest, of flesh from flesh, and one-two-three, the sky fell at last.

They all ended up in Sam and Eva's bed, squished together in a deep sleep. Rachel woke first and inspected them one by one to be sure they were all there and because she could: Leah couldn't boss her to mind her own business, her parents couldn't ask what was wrong. Now she understood that she'd wasted a lot of time ignoring Emma, whose cheeks were as smooth as the petals on a rose. The baby looked like Leah and people said she looked like Rachel too, but Rachel had never seen it before.

A new light shone in the room. Rachel slithered from bed and tiptoed barefoot through the kitchen, where the dishes from the night before were piled in the sink; the storm had defeated her mother's custom of making the kitchen spotless for the next day.

On the lawn there were leaves everywhere, not just the unmistakable maple leaves but the heart shapes of lilac leaves and the long fronds of ferns. Flowers, too: bee balm, roses, tiger lilies, pansies, pinks were scattered on the lawn in no pattern. The hem of Rachel's nightgown was soon bordered in wet blossoms.

Around the corner of the house, along the driveway, lay the giant maple. Its fractured roots reached into the air higher than four Rachels. The earth that had once held the tree in place perfumed the air with sharp misery.

The tree was down. The air and light always would be empty of it. In its place there would be nothing forever.

Rachel pushed her way along the tree trunk into the complicated branches until she reached the top of the giant maple.

She climbed onto a branch, and it rose and fell beneath her

weight. She looked beyond the outstretched arms of the tree. From where she stood, she could see past her sisters and herself, past Eva and Sam, the Ziegelmans and the Scotts, past the new baseball diamond where no one had played but where they would, past babies already born and one other, the last Scott baby, a girl, to a time when all this life of babies and children, summers and swimming, would be lost, all the people lost to each other. She could see her oldest happiness, the one that would disappear, and her greatest losses, the ones that would never be replaced.

Time was coming for them all. But not yet. It wasn't there yet.

The Hospital Room

There was Helen standing at the window, a soft figure against the light. The end-of-winter sun passed through the room high up on the sixth floor, through the bare branches—gray clouds, tall windows all day long. Helen's voice chorded with the drone of the street, and Eva strained to catch the words. If she didn't make some effort, she would be only eyes open to blurs, ears full of sound.

"Things change," Eva wanted to say.

"He's always been impossible. I should be grateful, right? That some things don't change. You always say that, Eva. I'm never sure if you're kidding. He says I have no sense of humor, so you might be kidding, and I'm so . . . What's the word he uses? *Gruesome.* How does Harris get to say *gruesome*? About me?"

She should turn. She should face the dear shrunken thing on the bed. These visits—she didn't visit often enough. The hospital was close, ten blocks up Fifth Avenue. That was close enough to come every day; that's what she should have been doing. In the country they drove miles to get together with the kids and they did it every day, so many summer afternoons spent by the pond, watching the children swim. Now they were in the city. Distances changed in the city.

"It's the kids I worry about," Helen said. "They're like you. They think that everything should stay the same, but it can't."

To be honest, Harris hadn't used the word about her but about the painting she'd bought last week, which was very beautiful.

Harris had said the painting was gruesome but it made her glad to be alive. He was too impatient to see that the forms resolved into the most glorious landscape, the fleeting ghost of a place you'd once loved. To imitate her looking at art, Harris squeezed his face together like someone with cramps. She walked to the Met. She could walk to her dear friend's hospital room.

It was possible that their country life was over.

Helen turned and moved toward the bed. "Did I tell you that I bought another painting last week?" She stood by Eva. "The same painter."

Eva tried to smile but her lips stayed together. Helen opened the jar of ointment on the bedside table, stuck her red-nailed pinky into it, and dotted Eva's lips. The nurses used a wooden stick. Helen pressed her lips together in sympathy, miming the way they used to try each other's lipsticks.

The bedside table was a mess. Helen sorted out pitcher, cup, straw. She added water to the half inch in the cup, replaced the pitcher, and held the cup with its crooked straw to Eva's mouth. She was no good at this. When the children were sick, Harris was the one to hold the cup at the right angle. Eva's lips parted; she sipped and turned away. Helen set the cup back on the bedside table and returned to her place at the window, relieved that she hadn't spilled anything on poor Eva.

She was a large woman, taller than Eva by half a foot, but Eva had been the stronger, tending her vegetable garden, doing her own laundry and cooking and the eternal cleaning. Now Eva couldn't hold her water cup in her own hand.

When Sam visited Eva in the evening, he reassured her that

everything was fine, as if he were delivering a memorized speech. A woman came in the afternoon to clean the apartment and cook dinner. She was there when the kids got home from school. Eva wouldn't think of that now. Helen's tweed suit was beautiful and her leather walking shoes well kept. The striped silk blouse echoed the colors in the tweed and the deep blue of her eyes. Her best feature. Helen had never been happy with her looks but she knew how to dress.

"I fell in love," Helen said. "Eva. What am I going to do?"

When Sam came in the evening after work, he reported that spring was coming. If she said, "Tell me," Sam looked stymied, then told her about the paperwhites and jonquils blooming in the enormous pots that flanked the hospital doors. She couldn't picture the doors, though she must have passed through them to get to this room. He told her that the kids wouldn't need their winter jackets much longer. The relief that came at the end of winter—no more gloves, scarves, and hats to be lost, no pile of melting boots and skates in the foyer. Any other year she'd have been planning what to take to the country; their weekends would resume after Passover. The annual questions had to be asked: What must be done to the house and how would they manage? Would the girls still be content with another summer of swimming at Helen's and sleepovers back and forth? Would their neighbor plow their garden in time for spring planting? Another life, more dream than memory. From the window at twilight Sam reported that the traffic moved slowly along Fifth Avenue: A big white dog lumbered past, pursued by a square little man.

She could picture the stone wall dividing the park from Fifth Avenue.

Eva's lips parted and she touched them with her tongue. Love, she meant to say, love was always wonderful, no matter, no matter, no penalty for love. This wasn't true. She wanted to say something that was true.

"It's an old story," Helen said.

A shadow floated across Helen. Midafternoon.

"It's . . . He's very simple. He's good. You see the goodness in his paintings. Not that they're simple—I'm not finding the right words."

Helen's neck bent. Her hands rose to her face. If Helen had been near, Eva would have made the effort to lift her hand to touch her. Too far away.

"Sweetie," Eva said.

Helen raised her head.

Rachel peeked in at the half-open door, her gaze passing from her mother in the bed to Helen at the window.

The girl's lean face was red from the wind and cold of the outside world. Her slip hung below the hem of her brown burlap wraparound skirt. One shoulder was weighed down by her dark green book bag.

How unlike Helen's own girls in their neat uniforms. But Rachel had always been like this, showing up in a bathing suit three sizes too big because she liked the color, or a shirt too small and full of holes because it was her favorite. Eva always said that Rachel danced to her own tune, and what did it matter what kids wore?

Eva raised and lowered a finger to her daughter.

Helen moved closer to the bed. "Sweetheart," she said. "How did you get here?"

"I took the bus," Rachel said.

"Of course," Helen said. "I forget how grown-up you are."

"I take two buses to school," Rachel said. "Crosstown and downtown. Sometimes the train."

On mornings when she dawdled too long at home she had to take the subway, where hands reached up under her skirt and she was smashed in and couldn't get away. Someday her lateness would have to be reckoned with, maybe as soon as the next report card.

She saw her mother's beckoning finger, and Rachel set her book bag next to the bed.

"Hi, Mom," Rachel said. She leaned over her mother, inhaling her mother's hospital smell.

"Rachel," Eva said.

The girl plopped herself down in the visitor's chair.

"School?" Eva asked.

"We're reading Chaucer." Rachel had decided what to report to please her mother. " 'Whan that Aprille with his shoures soote / The droughte of March hath perced to the roote.' We're supposed to memorize ten lines."

Something pressed in Eva's throat. She tried to swallow. Her mouth opened, and liquid rose, foaming, bilious. Rachel shoved her chair back, kicking her book bag away from the bed.

"Where's the button?" Helen asked. "Where's the nurse?"

Eva closed her eyes. The dizziness got worse. She had to keep breathing. Her mouth needed wiping, the floor needed cleaning, and she couldn't lift a finger.

There were bubbles in the yellow puddle. Rachel's mother was no longer her mother. *Look at her.* Other kids had a mother waiting in the kitchen when school was over to hand out cookies and milk, and ask, *How was school today?* The mothers who worked came in at the end of the day with briefcases and the *Times* folded up, and kicked off their high-heel shoes and called for their daughters.

Eva's eyes were closed.

"I'm no good at this," Helen said. She went to the bathroom and returned with a handful of paper towels, which she draped over the puddle.

Eva inhaled raggedly as if she weren't getting the air she needed.

"Where is that nurse?" Helen was at the door of the room, looking out into the dim and deserted hall. There was always someone in a hospital hall during visiting hours. What was wrong with everyone? It was so simple. Wipe the woman's mouth. Clean the floor.

Take Rachel away, Eva thought. *This isn't her business.*

As if she'd thought things through, Helen picked up her coat and handbag and said, "Eva. We're finding someone and we're going, dear. Rachel and I are leaving. I'll be back tomorrow."

Helen ushered Rachel from the hospital room, stopping at the elevator and commanding, "Rachel. Stay here." At the nurses' station, Helen said: "Get someone into Mrs. Cantor's room right away."

Outside, the air was chilly yet spring was a presence, moist and fragrant inside the cold.

"How will you get home?" Helen asked.

"The crosstown." Mrs. Ziegelman must know that. Or maybe she never took the bus. Rachel was glad for her company on the darkening avenue. "How's Betsey and Katie? Lily?"

"They're fine. They miss you. We'll have you and your sisters over soon."

And why didn't the two families get together in the city? One family on the West Side, one on the East Side, both in the nineties. They could walk across the park but they didn't. Her girls had their lessons after school, tennis, piano, art on Saturdays, riding on Thursday. The differences showed more in the city.

"Are you still taking ballet?" she asked Rachel.

"Three times a week."

"Isn't that wonderful," Helen said.

At the bus stop, Rachel said, "Well, good-bye." Helen meant to kiss her but missed her chance. She should invite Rachel over for dinner. Rachel was waving, turning and watching for the bus. Another time.

The crosstown bus swayed through the park like an old horse loping home. If only the stone wall around Central Park continued throughout the city to show the difference between one place and the next. Rachel liked it best when it rained and the ins and outs of the stones were in sharp relief. She would go inside one of them and stay, or maybe rest for a while. She wanted to believe that she knew each stone and would remember it always. She knew this wasn't true.

The visit today had been the shortest. If only it were Mrs. Ziegelman in the bed and her mother taking care of things. Her mother would do a good job, not like Mrs. Ziegelman. And not like herself. Rachel didn't know what to do except count the minutes until she could leave, and when she left there was no relief. She never stayed long enough. She never said the right thing. There must be rules for such a visit but she didn't know them. She had no stories to tell her mother besides school was fine, everything was fine at home. Her father had warned, *Don't worry your mother.*

Rachel didn't believe that her mother was in the hospital room, or that the room existed. It had to be only a matter of time before her mother would reappear and their lives would be once again as they had been.

Ahead, the stone wall at the park's western edge, almost the end of the ride.

The apartment door would open, and in would come her mother dragging a shopping cart behind her filled with bags of food, asking for a hand unloading, and saying, *Shut the door behind me, please.*

The little nurse's aide wiped Eva's face clean, took her blood pressure (the squeeze of the cuff troubled Eva), and checked her temperature. The room smelled of disinfectant, but that would pass. She pushed the visitor's chair back in place for the patient's husband, who came like clockwork every night. He liked to sit at his wife's side, the one without the IV. Around the room she moved, touching this, arranging that. The patient was motionless in the bed, eyes closed. *Poor thing, you're all filled up with the sickness. You've had just about enough, haven't you?* But the body was merciless and insisted on living.

The lights came on along the paths in the park, making the trees look stark and empty. The nurse's aide drew the curtains over the tall windows and left.

The hush returned to the hospital room. Old friend. Eva was in the garden, her summer garden with everything her family liked—tomatoes and corn, cucumbers, and potatoes—also floppy white orchids, the droopy kind women wore at weddings, and marble pillars coated with raucous pink hibiscus and dangling purple wisteria, flowers she'd seen before only on wallpaper, and they were flat like wallpaper, then not flat, flowers you could put your arms through if you could reach them. Summer, summer again. Beyond the garden, across a muzzy gray space, Eva spied water. Light was bouncing off the triangular waves, sparkling brilliantly. The children were out there in the water. They caught sight of her and rose in the air like fish, then fell back, covered with light, and they beckoned to her, to come join them in the water.

Helen walked more quickly as she neared home. Lily would be back from the park by now, perhaps sitting in the kitchen watching while dinner was prepared. She was a child who liked carrots. Maybe she was sitting and watching with a carrot in one hand. The older girls would be in their rooms either doing their homework or pretending to do it. They would eat with her and Harris, if he came home in time for dinner.

She'd felt wonderful on the way to the hospital, and she tried to remember what she'd felt so good about—not about seeing Eva. That she'd dreaded. Poor Rachel, this wasn't going to be easy for her.

In the park, all the lights came on at once, and the coincidence made Helen laugh. It was never wrong to love. If Eva were here, Helen was sure, she'd agree.

A breeze touched her coat collar and awakened a faint reminder of oil paint and turpentine in the wool. Cigarette smoke. And Scotch whiskey, that too. She'd see him in three days. Anticipation warmed her in the cool evening. His painting was so right. The floating forms on his canvas were a perfect gesture, like the park lights coming on. In a blink, everything fit together.

The Thief

I n my fifteenth year, a lifetime ago, I was far from here in New York City where I was born. We lived on the Upper West Side, then a graying neighborhood of European refugees and Puerto Rican immigrants, and my school was on the East Side, across the park and downtown thirty blocks or so. I took two buses to school, or one bus and a subway if it looked like I'd be late. My mother had died several years before, and my father had moved us recently to a new apartment, landing me in between my usual bus stops. Every morning going east to school, every afternoon coming home, I had to decide—Eighty-sixth? Ninety-sixth? *I have trouble making up my mind,* I told myself, practicing a smile that would express acceptance of my eccentricities. A girl in my Latin class had perfected a smile that was like a lost thought. When I smiled, my eyes disappeared and my funny upper teeth were exposed.

One rainy winter afternoon, I was on the Eighty-sixth Street crosstown, on my way home. As the bus swerved through the park, I put my book bag on the floor and elbowed a woman wearing a see-through raincoat. She gave me a dirty look. She was small, hunched, her white pageboy covered by a pleated plastic kerchief you knew she kept in her purse in the envelope it came in, just in case. At Central Park West, half the population pushed out while the other half held its ground. I lifted my book bag over my shoulder and scuffed the woman's foot in farewell. "Clumsy!" she cried out, and she was right. I was clumsy and eager to be outside.

West on Eighty-sixth through the rain and freezing air, almost to Broadway, past the scowling doorman, up in the elevator, at last I stood at the door to 8D, Caitlin's apartment. When I pressed the bell and the familiar notes sounded, no voice called out, no footsteps scuffed on the parquet floor, so I turned to ring for the elevator, resigned to going home.

The apartment door opened a crack, and Caitlin peeked out.

"Oh, Rachel," she said. "It's only you. Thank God."

We would never have been friends—Caitlin was a year older and went to a different school—except that, the summer before, we went to the same camp in Massachusetts. During afternoon drawing class we sneaked off to smoke in the woods, leaving behind the earnest campers with their pads of cheap paper, their pieces of charcoal, and the still life of weeds in a Mason jar. I admired the way Caitlin held her cigarette to her mouth, the way she rubbed ash into her dungarees to age them. Caitlin fieldstripped her butts, pulling apart the delicate paper seam and sprinkling the tobacco over the grass. It was a dry summer and everyone was always warning everyone else about fire. Caitlin and I were equally self-absorbed, but she more happily. Her face was heart shaped, her mouth like a rose, her eyes pale blue, and her hair nearly black. There was a glow to her skin, slightly unreal, that made you want to touch her.

Caitlin led the way down the wide hall. In her bedroom, her white ruffled quilt and pillows slumped half off the mattress, the books were flung faceup and facedown, spines cracked. Caitlin's china ballerinas were scattered on the blue carpet, arms snapped off at the shoulders. The closet door was open, her clothes tumbled out on the floor. A single blouse clung to its hanger. Even the framed reproductions of Degas ballerinas hung crooked on the walls.

I decided not to mention the state of the room.

"Crummy day," I said. "I hate March." I slipped off my loafers and dropped my raincoat on top of them.

"That's going to make a nice puddle. Oh, leave it alone. You can never do anything right around here anyway." Caitlin flopped on the bed. "Bobby's gone," she said, and she giggled. "Gone, man. Gone."

"Really?"

"I guess *really*. Look what he did to my room."

At our camp, Bobby worked in the kitchen along with the Nigerian scholarship students, washing dishes, serving vats of food. Bobby was a year older than Caitlin and had a certain glamour; he had a job for the summer and wasn't just another camper. Off duty, he wore jeans and a white T-shirt tight enough to show off his muscles. He stuck his pack of cigarettes in the cuff of his T-shirt, and he slicked his hair back like a movie gangster's. Winter was less kind to Bobby. The subway ride from Queens to Caitlin's apartment on the Upper West Side seemed to wear him down. At least, he was always in a bad mood when I saw him.

When Bobby was there, I didn't stay long. When I dropped by after school, or when Caitlin and I had a date and Bobby should have been the third wheel, they weren't interested in me, and he didn't bother to hide it. Sometimes Caitlin and Bobby passed a cigarette back and forth silently, and the air filled with their smoke. Then I'd tiptoe to the apartment door, travel down in the elevator counting to ten over and over, and explode into the outside air like I'd escaped.

Caitlin laughed, making a sound as if someone were strangling her. "This is the straw that broke the camel's back, as my mother would cliché. I broke up with him. For real this time in case you want to ask. So he trashed my room. And he—" Caitlin looked around the way she did when she wanted a cigarette. The smudge on her right cheek might have been blue-gray eye shadow. A red mark glowed beneath the tender skin.

Other times I'd noticed bruises on Caitlin. Once I tapped her on the shoulder to get her attention, and she winced like I'd found a sore spot. Caitlin never talked to me about the bruises, and I didn't ask her.

Looking around the room, I felt sure of myself for the first time in Caitlin's company. I was the neat one and my parents and sisters were messy; it was the theme of family jokes and hadn't seemed like a bad thing until my mother died and it was just me and my father and sisters. Now my older sister was away at college, and my little sister was staying that year with our aunt in Pennsylvania, so it was just me and my father.

"Do you want me to help you clean up?" I asked. "It won't take long—"

"That way—" Caitlin flicked a glance at the broken dancers.

"That way what?"

"No one's going to know what he did."

Having secrets and keeping them were nothing but a burden to me, who had nothing to hide. I began setting the books in piles, and I worked quickly, absorbed in seeing which ones I'd read, when I heard Caitlin giggling.

"What?" I asked.

"The books."

"Oh. I like them alphabetized. That way, you can always find them."

"Don't stop! It's just funny."

Slowly, Caitlin collected cigarette butts from the floor and lobbed them at the red metal wastebasket, missing only once. Barefoot, she rubbed ashes into the patterned carpet.

"There," she said.

When the books were in place, I remade the bed and plumped the eiderdown. While Caitlin straightened the pictures on the walls, I arranged the porcelain corps de ballet on the floor, the broken dancers on their backs in a line. Someone had taken trouble with the ballerinas, really thought about the way a dancer's arm curved. I touched my finger to a hand and stroked the chilly palm.

"Keep the one in the pink tutu," Caitlin said. "Get rid of the rest." She leaned over and dropped the limbs and trunks in with the cigarette butts. "I'll do the clothes," she said. "You empty the wastebasket. You'll see where."

The butler's pantry was lined with glass-fronted cabinets, two, three patterns of china, and crystal of all kinds, arranged in rows. My parents had two sets of china, everyday and good; we used the good twice a year for Thanksgiving and Passover. Looking at the cabinets, it occurred to me that Caitlin's family lived a life so different from my own, it might as well have taken place in one of the thin novels I loved, about England before World War I, when everything went wrong.

On the way back to Caitlin's room, I stopped at the dining room. The table was covered by a white tablecloth, at each place crystal saltcellars and tiny mountains of spilled salt, as if the table had been left since the night or even nights before. Once I'd stayed for dinner. Caitlin's father, who had a crew cut and wore a bow tie, brought his whiskey to the table and set it next to his wine-glass. Her mother, prettier than Caitlin, her skin even creamier, drank wine and ran a red nail along the tablecloth. When everyone else was finished eating, she put a forkful of food into her mouth, chewed, swallowed, and said, "There. That's over," as if we'd survived a stormy ocean voyage. A broad dark-skinned woman with graying hair, Ivy, worked for the family. The night I stayed for dinner she waited in the kitchen while we ate. When Caitlin's mother rang a silver bell by her plate, Ivy wheeled a cart to the table, loaded the dirty plates onto one shelf, served dessert from another, and disappeared into the kitchen.

Down the hall the parents' bedroom had the hush of a room that's just been cleaned. The bed was perfectly flat. Heavy drapes hung in identical folds, allowing only a single shaft of rainy light. Still holding Caitlin's wastebasket, I stepped into the room. Soft gray carpet sank under my feet. A round mirror hung from the opposite wall, and I moved closer to see myself in it. A pile of whiteness on the waxed mahogany vanity caught the light. I put down the basket and lifted the strand of cool heavy pearls. I'd heard that you bite pearls to test if they're real, but without putting them in my mouth I could tell that they were more real than anything else I'd ever seen. Each white globe was dimpled. Mysterious shadows formed in the crevasses.

The phone rang, startling me, and I heard Caitlin's voice two doors down. I backed out of the room, pulling the wastebasket behind me to cover my tracks in the carpet.

Caitlin lay on her bed. The phone, cradled, rested on her stomach. She was smiling but didn't say who'd called. Naturally, I wanted to know who it was and if Bobby was gone, gone, as Caitlin had said.

"Stay for dinner?" she asked, but she didn't mean it.

"I can't tonight," I said. "I'm meeting my father—" But Caitlin wasn't listening. She was waiting for me to leave so she could get back to her phone call. That was how I knew it was Bobby. As soon as she got rid of me, he'd be over.

I considered warning Caitlin to cover the mark under her eye. Her parents might notice it, and she'd be left explaining a lot of things she'd rather not.

I said, "Don't worry. No one's going to know anything."

"I'm not worried," Caitlin said.

On various occasions during my childhood, my father tried to impress on me his father's heroism in leaving Russia to cross a continent and an ocean to reach the United States. In elementary school, we'd learned about the immigrant groups that washed up in New York harbor, and we were encouraged to tell stories about where we came from. Most of us were first- or second-generation Americans. To be asked where we came from added a shameful confusion to what was supposed to be a lesson in patriotism.

When Grandpa made his voyage, he was younger than I was that night, hurrying to meet my father in the garment district, at his favorite restaurant with its famous service from cranky elderly waiters. At the fish restaurant, which never changed, the tables were covered with stiff, much-laundered white cloths. My father liked eating before the dinner rush, and when I arrived, frozen and breathless, the place was nearly empty. That early in the evening, the hexagonal tiles on the floor gave off a faint odor of mop water and bleach. The mirrors lining the walls and the sparkling glass of the front window made the restaurant look bigger than it really was, two, even three times bigger.

"Your grandfather worked in the garment center in the Depression. Once in a great while, he came to this restaurant for oysters on the half shell. I swear some of the waiters were working here then. Busboys. You don't eat oysters, right? Not old enough. Someday you'll like them."

"I like them fried. Or is that clams?"

"You like fried clams, sugar," he said. "Remember the clams?"

Three summers before, my mother's sister let us have the house on Martha's Vineyard that she rented for two weeks every July; it had taken nothing less than a heart attack to stop her from coming. Every day we ate fried clams from a stand in Menemsha, and then my mother lounged on the back porch overlooking the bay and read her mysteries. In the fall, she would go to the doctor with a swelling in her abdomen, feeling more tired than she ever had, and it would be our disaster—although none of us knew that.

He ordered a half bottle of wine and a baked flounder. When he finished eating one side, he showed me how to turn the fish to get to the other side while keeping the spine intact: "Voilà!" he said, laughing a little loudly. His success with the flounder impressed me. My clumsiness came from his side of the family. We were always bumping into doorjambs and dropping glasses. My father was tall in those days, with eyebrows about to get bushy and eyes that showed every feeling he had. That night, he was decades younger than I am now. He was considered handsome though I saw only his fears and worries. He had long arms and legs; my mother said that he couldn't walk down the street without stepping on everyone else's feet.

My fried clams were served on an oval platter with fries and coleslaw, and I drank ginger ale, getting a kick out of the bubbles when they hit my nose.

"I have some news for you," my father said. He pushed back from the table. Full, happy, he lit one of the smelly cigars he liked so much.

I put down my fork and wiped my mouth carefully.

"There," I said. "That's over."

"Rachel," my father said. "Honey. There's someone I want you to meet."

"For real?" I asked, but I knew it was. He'd been dating someone, the same person, someone he'd known a million years ago and then—he wouldn't have made this special occasion at the fish restaurant if he wasn't going to do something about her. With her.

I raised my glass of ginger ale and said, "I hope you'll be happy, Daddy." It was what a girl in a movie would do and it was what I did because he looked so miserable telling me. I thought, *Last nail, last nail in my mother's coffin.*

After our traditional dessert of blueberry pie à la mode, we took a cab uptown instead of the subway, proving that this was an occasion. My father hailed the cab in the way only natives do, his raised arm casual, peremptory, even a little theatrical.

The move to the new, bigger apartment made sense now.

Maybe we'd be happy, I thought, or happier than we were now. That was what my father must have believed. He was moving in the direction of his own happiness, leaving my sisters and me behind, whether he knew it or not.

When my father and I got home from the restaurant, we settled in the living room, he on the couch, I in the big chair with my Latin text and notebook on my lap, my feet on the ottoman.

My mother sang show tunes around the house, but that was the extent of her musical interest. My father and I listened to the opera on the radio every Saturday afternoon, and once he took me to City Center to *The Magic Flute*. He was musical; he had a beloved collection of Dixieland and original cast recordings, and some scratchy old Chopin. Even I was more musical than my mother. I loved the Brahms First Concerto for Piano and Orchestra. In our old apartment, our real apartment, I used to lie on the living room floor after my parents had gone to their bedroom, and I'd listen to the swelling strings and the corrective, meditative piano.

The new living room looked a lot better a month later when we unpacked the boxes of books and hung the pictures that leaned crookedly this way and that against the walls, but that night the chaos was an ocean surrounding our island of peace—the sofa, the chair, my father and I. He put on the Brahms I loved, a gesture I appreciated only in memory.

When the phone rang in the kitchen, we stared at each other until he said, "Go! Get it!" though he got to the phone first. Maybe it was someone he wanted me to meet. I knew I should go away and give him privacy, but I stayed.

"Hello," my father said. "Yes. This is Sam Cantor."

His eyes on me, he reached out his hand, groping on the counter for a pad and pencil.

If the phone hadn't rung, I thought, *we'd still be sitting in the quiet.*

"Tomorrow? You say tomorrow?" A woman's voice whined from the phone like a mosquito. "That's a shame. I can't be there. I have to catch an early train. I have a meeting in Boston. You don't understand. No. Look, is this an emergency? Can't we meet day after tomorrow? Tomorrow night?" My father was an accommodating man by nature. It was just a matter of time before he gave in. He frowned and said my name, "Rachel," not to me but to whoever was calling. "Lawyer? That's not necessary at this stage, is it?"

After he hung up the phone, he stood looking at it, and he didn't speak while I trailed him back to the living room. Again, he took the sofa and I the chair.

"You have a friend," he said. "Caitlin?"

"From camp," I said.

"Irish girl?"

"Jewish. Like everyone else at camp."

"Not that it matters," my father said.

"I don't know."

Let's talk about this subject, I wanted to say, *let's talk about it,* anything to slow down our conversation, to slow it enough to reverse the universe.

"It seems," my father said, "that when your friend Caitlin's mother came home from work, she went looking for her pearls. They were going to an affair. But she couldn't find them."

He kept his eyes on me.

Caitlin's lovely, slim mother was in her bedroom, her black suit discarded. Her sturdy black pumps from her office costume were cast aside. Silver dancing shoes awaited her, a match for the soft gray gown spread out on the bed. But where were her pearls?

"Real pearls," said my father. "Not cultured. You know the difference? What do these people do anyway?"

Caitlin said something once about her mother's job but she'd acted so bored by the topic that I didn't dare to press for details.

"Caitlin's mother works in an ad agency. Or architecture," I said. "And her father's in some kind of business. His office is on Park Avenue."

"They want to talk to you."

"What about?"

"About the pearls," he said. "Haven't you been listening to me?"

"I don't know what you're saying."

"With someone official, like this insurance investigator guy," he said, "you answer questions. You maintain a polite attitude."

"Investigator?"

"Their insurance company is investigating. Why can't you listen? This is so complicated?"

He was shouting at me, the way he had since my mother died: A damp bath towel left on my bedroom floor. Dishes in the sink, which I was going to wash. The Brahms playing over and over. My posture, which he said would play hell with my skeleton as I aged. My looks, which were not up to my mother's. He once left me twenty dollars and a note telling me to get a haircut, but I didn't touch the money. My mother got her hair cut in the East Forties but I didn't know where.

"What am I supposed to do?" I shouted back. "What am I supposed to do?"

He calmed to the temperature of ice.

"Lower your voice, for a start. You'll go to their apartment tomorrow after school. A person from the insurance company will be waiting for you."

"But I don't know anything."

"The girl claims you were there today," he said. "Your friend Caitlin."

"I dropped by—"

"And that some things were broken. Some kind of little figurines. The mother said she found the pieces."

"I didn't break anything."

"Good. If you're innocent," he said, "you have nothing to fear."

"But what should I say?"

"Rachel. Pay attention. Believe me, these people are insured. They have to do this, this formality. Then they'll get their money. Don't worry about it. It's just for show."

He seemed so sure of himself that I could tell there was no use arguing.

"When tomorrow?"

"I told you. After school. Are you listening, Rachel?"

In our family, most things became a joke, once enough time had passed. Not this. My father never mentioned it again. Once he was dead, many years later, I came to wonder if it ever happened.

The next afternoon, I again took the Eighty-sixth Street crosstown to Central Park West, walked to Broadway, crossed the lobby past the scowling doorman, and went up in the elevator to the eighth floor. This time when I rang the bell Caitlin's mother opened the door. She wore a gray tweed suit with little flecks of red and blue, and red pumps with very high heels. Underneath the suit was a ruffled satin blouse.

"Oh," she said, and let me inside. Without offering to take my raincoat or book bag, she led me down the hall. As I passed, I glanced into Caitlin's room. There was no sign of Caitlin, and her room looked remarkably neater than we'd made it the day before.

In the dining room, the table was bare. The crystal saltcellars were lined up on the sideboard. A man sat at the table, a file folder open before him. Balding, a little fleshy, he resembled Julius Caesar. *Veni, vidi, vici.*

Caitlin's mother said, "Rachel, this is Mr. Martino."

"Have a seat." His eyes on his file, he indicated a chair two away from his own.

"Her father?"

He looked up.

Caitlin's mother shrugged.

"He's in Boston," I said. "At a meeting. Otherwise . . ." Though it hadn't occurred to me that they expected my father to be with me.

"That's fine," he said. "You and I will be fine."

Caitlin's mother watched as I found the chair he'd indicated. My legs would barely bend to let me sit.

She said, "Just answer his questions, Rachel."

When the sound of her footsteps died out in the hallway, Mr. Martino said, "Fine. So. You met Caitlin at camp?"

"Yes."

"In Massachusetts."

"Yes. In Massachusetts."

"And you visit her after school?"

"Yes."

"You come often?"

I squinted at him, wondering what Caitlin had said.

"Sometimes."

"Fine." His favorite word. "This where you live?" He picked a piece of paper out of the folder and tilted it toward me.

"No," I said. "We moved."

"Since when?" He seemed annoyed with me.

"A few months ago."

Mr. Martino said, "I hear that your mother died."

"A few years ago. Three."

"I'm sorry," Mr. Martino said.

He wrote my new address down and drew careful lines through my old one, so straight I would have guessed he'd used a ruler.

"So. You're on your own after school. So sometimes you don't feel like going home and you visit your friend Caitlin from camp?"

"Yes."

"Nice apartment," Martino said. "Nice setup."

For the first time, I noticed the etchings of fruit framed in thin black wood. The sideboard's doors and drawer-fronts were carved with bunches of grapes and twisted vines.

"Sometimes," Martino said, smiling, "when we don't have what we want, we feel like other people have too much. You know what I mean?"

I tried to smile too but couldn't make my lips go up.

"Kids take things, Rachel," he said, and now his voice was low, as if he didn't want anyone else to hear, though no one else was listening. "It's a phase. No big deal. You see what I mean?"

He was waiting for me to speak. From long practice, I knew that if I withstood the torture of silence, grown-ups filled in the blanks.

"You see, Rachel, no one else was here yesterday but you. The pearls, they're worth a lot of money. Your friend's parents want them back, and they're going to get them. So it really isn't worth it to keep them. What's a kid going to do with pearls like that?"

"I didn't take anything," I said.

He sighed, touched his ear, and continued his study of the piece of paper with my address.

"So you drop by yesterday. Unannounced. You visit your friend Caitlin. What do two girls your age do?"

"She's a year older than I am," I said.

"So she's a special friend."

For a second, I believed that Caitlin had told Mr. Martino that I was her special friend.

"That's a phase, too," he said. "It can go along with stealing."

"What can?" I asked, because I didn't know what he was talking about, and his face pinkened. He had hard blue eyes, and I wondered if he was wearing contacts like the girl next to me in history.

"Friendships," he said. "The special ones."

"I didn't take anything," I said.

It seemed silly to lie. It was bound to come out that I was nothing special to Caitlin. Sitting there, I knew that we'd never be friends again, and that in truth we never had been.

There was a knock at the door. Caitlin's mother had changed; she wore slim pants and a black V-neck sweater that showed the edge of her lace bra. Her bare neck rose from the sweater.

"How's it going?" she asked.

"Fine," Mr. Martino said. "Rachel here is just about ready to go home."

"That's good," said Caitlin's mother. "People are coming for dinner."

"Fine," he said. "I'll see Rachel out," as if I couldn't be trusted to leave on my own.

"Good-bye, Rachel." Her voice spoke a final farewell, like she was dropping me at a train station.

The whole eight floors down, Mr. Martino and I kept our eyes on the numbers as they lit up in descending order. When the elevator stopped, he followed me into the lobby. The doorman was nowhere to be seen.

"You sure you don't have anything to tell me?" Mr. Martino asked. "About smoking dope, for example? Breaking other people's property? That's a phase, too. Kids break stuff when they get mad. They take stuff."

I could see my hand setting the pearls back on Caitlin's mother's vanity. Their coolness was no longer in my palm, and they lay there, glowing.

But at that moment I wondered, and sometimes I still do, if I did take the pearls. If so, where are they? If this were a fairy tale, I'd grind the pearls up into a powder, go to the underworld, and feed them to my mother.

I walked across the cool marble lobby, feeling Mr. Martino's eyes on me. I told myself not to turn around, but as I opened the heavy glass door, I couldn't help it.

He was waiting, his back to me, his eyes raised, watching the numbers. I waited also, hoping that when the elevator doors parted, someone I loved would emerge, walk straight past Mr. Martino and across the lobby to embrace me.

When the elevator came, I turned and left the building, out onto Eighty-sixth Street and into the rest of my life.

SECOND TRIO

A Thousand Words

Here It Was, November

The Blue Wall

A Thousand Words

Our daughter visited often during Per's swift and irreversible illness; now she was flying to the top of Vermont once more. Her plane landed on time at our little airport. When I saw her bright red hair, my heart lifted, that old balloon, and I forgot for a moment that Per was gone.

While we waited for her luggage, Astrid chastised herself for being such a heavy packer, a small fault in the greater scheme, though I agreed with her that it was a nuisance, and I wondered why anyone would want so much for two days, three at the most. She'd always been like that, as I didn't bother to remind her. I used to be like that myself.

In the car, Astrid said, "I made a list. All the people we need to call. Where and when we'll have the funeral."

"He wanted to be cremated. A few words and that's all. He didn't want a funeral. People having to come all the way."

"But what about his friends? People need closure, Mama."

"People need a lot of things," I said. It wasn't a time when I cared what anyone else needed. Astrid went ahead with her plans.

For the next week I played my part and received Per's students and colleagues—he'd died *in medias res* as he was about to retire—a few enemies; many friends; his agent, editor, and other dignitaries from the world of letters; and a cousin sent from Stockholm to represent the family. To everyone's disappointment, he was a tall, blond, blue-eyed Swede, nothing like Per.

Astrid dreamed up a ceremony, and lilies of the valley—every bloom in the garden—covered the casket. Per died too soon for red lilacs, his favorite color never seen that spring. Lilies of the valley were all I had for him. The pall was a cloth he'd brought home from a trip to West Africa. It was rough, simple, the color of wheat, handwoven, very beautiful. The market women sewed four pieces together to make a cover for our wide bed. In the grange hall, the cloth was draped over his casket. Everybody touched it as they passed.

A friend who'd once been a famous singer played a guitar someone loaned her and sang a ballad I hadn't heard in years. Then came the Twenty-third Psalm with its darling sheep and generous meal; "Stop all the clocks . . . ," a poem Auden hated; an early love poem I'd written for Per—all read beautifully by our old friends. Astrid had made up a program, which the town secretary printed for her on ivory paper. Afterward, everyone regathered at our house, and Per— lilies of the valley, cloth, and all—was driven to the crematorium.

That was the way it would be from now on, I saw, Per in another place entirely.

A friend who'd come all the way from Baltimore decided that she couldn't bear to leave me alone, and she declared that she'd stay for one week, two weeks, but I persuaded her that her husband and students needed her more, and that with all of Per's traveling, I was used to being alone; this argument convinced her as the truth wouldn't have.

The Swedish cousin was the last to go, staying a day longer even than Astrid. The cousin's English was excellent but we had nothing to say to each other. He ate the meals I made for him. One afternoon he took a long walk to town and back. In the evening he talked about Per's books that were translated into Swedish. He kept saying, "back into Swedish," though they'd been written in English. Per had left Sweden just after his eighteenth birthday. After I ran Per's cousin to the airport and waited with him for his plane, I turned my faithful car around, drove home, and slept for twenty hours.

After a few weeks I discovered a routine: wake up, go back to sleep, wake up, and get to work.

The week before Per fell ill so unexpectedly and so disastrously, I'd accepted an assignment for my first prose piece in years, tempted into it by a former student of Per's, now the editor of a travel magazine, who wanted me to reminisce about New Mexico. Post-Lawrence, pre-now, he said, a thousand words, though I told him that I wouldn't know what *now* was like. And in all honesty, I didn't know what the place was like *then,* I only knew our life there.

"So many words!" Per said when I told him that I'd accepted the commission. Like so much of our conversation, the phrase echoed something said a hundred years ago. *So many words!* a poet had exclaimed when Per's second and most successful novel won so much acclaim and so many awards.

My little memoir was about the first place Per and I lived as man and wife, an adobe built in the Mexican style in the mountains close to Santa Fe. We'd rented it sight unseen for a song, the only one we could afford to sing. The house was furnished simply with heavy wooden furniture and bright cloth from Old Mexico, and it had everything we needed: kitchen, bedroom, two workrooms, even indoor plumbing, though we were young and thought we shouldn't be fussy.

We were there a month or more before we met our nearest neighbors, though sometimes in the evening we'd hear laughter or a car starting. I was in the courtyard one day around noon, sticking my pale calves into the sun, when I heard a noise from inside the house. Per was in town getting groceries and it seemed too soon for him to be home. Then a woman's voice calling, "Hello? Hello?" That's how it was that Marian Foster Todd stood in my house before I knew her name.

The world knows that Marian was more famous for being beautiful than she was for writing beautifully, and she was justifiably famous for that. For years, she was considered the best female American literary novelist, and she admitted freely that her beauty helped. Had Marian been in show business or fashion—fields where beauty really means something—no fuss would have been made about her conventional and pleasing looks, but that's the way of the world. Women who are not beautiful themselves can appreciate what the rest of the world values, and I always took pleasure in looking at Marian.

That day she wasn't yet famous or even published. She was dressed in an embroidered Mexican blouse, off the shoulders, and white pants that ended above her ankles. On her feet, she wore espadrilles, powdery lavender, a color never seen before or since. When she was settled in a lounge chair in the shade, a glass of iced tea in her hand, Marian explained that she was there from Santa Fe for the weekend, the guest of our neighbors, had walked too far, gotten turned around, and she had no idea where she was. Marian said this as if it were the most obvious thing in the world, though the houses were no farther apart than a quarter mile and the dusty road between them was as clear as day. We laughed as if we two were the only ones in the world who would find her predicament funny, and our friendship commenced. Laughter is the hardest thing of all to explain, after love.

We loved her, Per and I, and so did our daughter. Astrid called her Aunt Marian when she came to Vermont after we settled there for good, and Marian sent our daughter the most elaborate gifts. In those days, Marian had no money but that didn't stop her from spending it. Astrid kept the ribbons from Aunt Marian's gifts in a special box. The expense of the gifts troubled me but Per reminded me that Marian wasn't as lucky as we were and had no child of her own.

When Astrid was a very young child, it was at first difficult and finally impossible for me to be away from her. Accompanying Per to his many readings and lectures became painful; if our car burned or our plane crashed, if any harm came to us, our child would be orphaned. Once I suggested to Per that, in case he and I died together, Marian should be Astrid's guardian. Per shook his head. No matter how I pressed him to explain, he wouldn't discuss the matter and finally I dropped my idea. We fell into the habit of being apart; he traveled and I stayed with Astrid. At the end of the journey, he always came home, and I was always happy to see him.

Writing about the beginning of our marriage was better than answering condolence cards or trying to gather papers for the lawyer. Unlike the unwelcome memories of Per as he went to his death, my reminiscences of New Mexico offered the pleasure of rediscovery. I hadn't thought about that time or place for years, the way our house overlooked the valley of scrub oaks and junipers, and the rocks, lots of rocks, and the caves that appeared at certain angles of sunlight, then disappeared. A photographer was our closest neighbor in the hills beyond Santa Fe; his young boyfriend worked at a hardware store in the city. The boyfriend had grown up in Santa Fe, and he complained bitterly about how wonderful it had been before the war, how corrupted—how changed—it was now, how nothing was real anymore. Per thought he was silly but I tried to be friendly. He was young and out of his element in our circle, as we were in his.

One morning as I was remembering, the phone rang, and when I heard Marian's voice I wasn't surprised though I hadn't spoken to her in years. Others had called, friends who'd become strangers and those who'd missed the obituaries in the London, Stockholm, and New York papers but saw the appraisal of Per's work in *The New York Review of Books*. They asked me questions they imagined were original and tactful but they presumed on former intimacies: Was it painful? Did Per try this treatment or that? Had I heard that aloe vera was a cure for cancer? And why the caller hadn't visited/telephoned/written earlier: Some didn't want to bother me. Some were out of the country. One said that he was too self-absorbed. Marian didn't apologize or make excuses.

Because I'd been writing about Santa Fe (so many words! two hundred so far), Marian seemed close to my heart, closer than she'd been in fact for three decades. Per saw her more often than I. Once in a while, when he came home from being abroad or in New York, he'd report that he'd seen her and that she sent her love to me.

Marian wanted to come to Vermont to comfort me. I said I'd check my schedule and call her back. My caution was reflexive; over the years I'd guarded Per from the many pilgrims who wished to pay him homage.

If Per were there, he would ask, as he had other times: Why on earth did I want to see Marian? Didn't I remember how demanding she was, always insisting that if she ate this or that she'd have an allergic reaction and die so that I had to make special dishes catered to her taste, and how she'd insist on needing to iron her clothes but then she'd burn something and I'd volunteer to take over? Marian came first, her needs, her whims, her presence. Not a month past his death, past the months of illness and the days of dying, did I need someone else to care for? Why didn't I get on with the business of grieving or finish the piece for the magazine and earn a little money, or, best of all, write a poem? As his death should have taught me, there wasn't time to waste.

Marian's phone was busy when I called back but later she answered and sounded really delighted to hear that she was welcome to visit.

By this time the lilacs were almost gone and I was glad. Their odor—that fresh and mothballed scent—made me weep, and I resented my tears. Lilacs had always been my favorite flower. Would I now associate the look and smell of lilacs with Per's absence?

Marian chose Memorial Day weekend for her visit, and she claimed that she didn't drive, though how could anyone grow up in New Mexico and not know how to drive? I'd always suspected that she was a perfectly good driver but preferred being driven. In any case, she couldn't drive from New York, where she was then living, all the way to the top of Vermont. She scorned the bus and the train took forever. She would have to fly. Knowing her perpetual financial crisis, I made the reservation and paid for the ticket.

The day before her flight, Marian called to say that after all Memorial Day wasn't a good time for her to leave the city. There was so much to do. Someone at *Vogue* had approached her about a bimonthly column, which would give her a steady income and save her just when she really needed it. Mid-June, she said, when the peonies were in bloom, nothing would stand in her way. What did I want her to bring from the city? Marian suggested many presents that she couldn't possibly afford. When she decided that I had to have a baby pillow from Porthault with blue forget-me-nots on the case, I said, "Yes, just the thing," to stanch her guilty bleeding.

Marian was as full of promises as ever, and I as much of a fool for feeling disappointed that I wouldn't have her company right away. We were both in our sixties, I close to seventy. In my life, I'd written two collections of poems. My first book had been in print for forty years and my second for thirty. Someday I would have enough for a final volume. Marian was well known, but even at her age she was fiercely ambitious. She wanted the world to sit up straighter and to take even more note of her. She wanted more. *More* was the principle of her being, and it always had been.

What use was there in expecting her to change? As soon ask the cardinal outside my window to stop being red.

*   *   *

Now my article was five hundred words long, poet's words, which bottled the air of New Mexico and the altitude. Every night Per and I had such vivid dreams there and such pleasure in the morning when we told them. Years later to hurt my feelings Per said that he'd invented his.

Around this time, I reconsidered the wisdom of including Marian in my little essay. It was one thing to recall myself as a young poet, my husband as a young novelist, even to mention our neighbor the photographer, now renowned and dead. Before we left New Mexico, we bought a print from him of the view across the valley, and for the duration of our long marriage the photograph hung in our bedroom; I composed two sentences about his continued presence through the image taken so long ago. Writing about Marian would set our experience in the category of group memoir and imply that our happiness, Per's and mine, was communal or even social. After a few days, I was sure it was the right thing not to mention her at all. True, we'd met her while we were living in the adobe house but we could have met her anywhere.

Writing about that time made me realize how long ago it really was and helped me calculate how little of Marian I'd seen over the years. From New Mexico Marian moved to New York. We moved to New York and she moved to Paris. We moved to Baltimore, then to Vermont, and here we stayed. After Mexico City and California, Marian moved back to New York, and we intended to resume our friendship, she and I. Many times, she called to say that she was coming and I prepared for her visits as for a holiday, but Marian's circumstances intervened almost every time. She canceled with such elaborate regrets that I became embarrassed at my presumption in expecting her. I forgot my discomfort and disappointment quickly in my relief that daily life could continue uninterrupted. For years I paid little attention to anything other than Per and Astrid and the poems I wrote so slowly. Marian's promised visits and her projections of the wonderful time we'd have together were better than if she'd actually arrived with her complicating presence.

Astrid called at the last minute to say she was coming up for the Fourth of July, and once more I picked her up at the airport. In Per's day, when guests arrived he'd ask first thing, *How long exactly do we have you here with us?* I knew without asking that Astrid's visit would be brief though her luggage was the same as it had been for the week of Per's funeral. On the drive home, Astrid and I noted the changes that time had brought. She hated the few new houses built along the road. How could they have done it? Why did the houses have to be so ugly? Why aluminum siding? Though I'd had such thoughts myself, I said, "It's practical, sweetie. They won't ever have to paint."

Astrid had none of the virtues of my side of the family—height, broad shoulders, straight thick hair. Rather, she looked like Per's mother, small, lovely, with red hair that had a life of its own. Today it wanted to elope with the breeze from the open window.

When she was a child, Astrid so loved being with me that I used to worry that Per would feel left out. When she became a teenager, things changed and stayed that way. Per was the reason she came home from college, he with whom she took long walks, he to whom she sent books she wanted to share. Once in a while, she hugged me, and I tried to interpret in her gesture the longing that I felt for our old companionable times. Astrid developed the notion that I didn't appreciate Per as an artist or a human being, and that I never understood what he wanted and needed. When she spoke about the ways in which I fell short as the wife of a great man, I saw white; my ears rang, my blood roped in my forehead. Now that Per was dead, he was both simpler and larger. He had a beginning, middle, and end. Driving home with Astrid, I thought that perhaps I did see him too narrowly.

"Let's get rid of Dad's things," Astrid said. "Clean out his study. Give away his clothes."

"Start all the clocks," I said.

"Don't think of it that way, Mama. It won't interfere with the process of mourning," she said. "It won't change anything except it helps you face the truth."

"What makes you think I don't already?" I asked.

"It makes it a lot worse to let the stuff sit around and have to do it later. Better to do it now."

The tears in my eyes shamed me.

"And where did you learn this wisdom?" I asked. "A how-to book on grief?"

"An old friend of yours. *Who* it is doesn't matter."

"Who is it?"

Who was talking to my daughter when I wasn't, who was with her while I was hundreds of miles away, waiting for each day to pass?

"Aunt Marian was so worried. She always thought that—"

"You saw her."

"She called. After the funeral. To say she was so sorry."

"Marian always thought *what*?"

"Oh, nothing, Mama. Marian wanted to come this weekend to help us, but she's preparing for some conference or something in New Mexico. In her honor. They're naming a new library after her. She was born there, you know."

"Yes, that's where we—"

"She's going to Albuquerque. I've never been there."

Astrid might have been, for on our way out of New Mexico, Per and I stayed the night in a white stucco motel on Route 66, and a month later I discovered that I was pregnant.

Early on in our friendship, Marian cautioned me. "You have to be more careful. You don't understand the world. People aren't nice." She dispensed the advice though I was older than she, married, had had a poem in *The New Yorker* (ten lyric lines), and she was just starting on her way.

Our neighbor kicked Marian out one weekend, either because

he imagined that she was flirting with his boyfriend or because he had good reason to be sure. And so she came to us, "for sanctuary," she claimed, and spent the night in our living room. In the morning we woke to the smell of pancakes and coffee, and later Per drove her back to her casita near the square in Santa Fe. The next time she came out to the mountains it was as our guest, and she and I giggled when we walked past the photographer's house. She confided to me that she wanted more than anything to go to New York, to a bigger arena for the life she wanted.

One day, right after she'd been with us for a weekend, Marian phoned and asked me to go to the photographer's to retrieve a bracelet she'd left in his guest room. When I got there and explained what I wanted, he was polite and a bit puzzled. He followed me to the guest room and watched as I looked for the bracelet, which was nowhere to be found. Perhaps I imagined it, but he was distant after that, and our friendship dwindled. He was a very nice man and walked me back to my house, though it was the heat of the afternoon.

Marian was wrong about me. I wasn't tolerant or kind by nature. I wasn't that interested in people, not the way she was. When I was a little girl I had an awful temper but it got me nowhere so I learned quieter ways to live and get what I wanted. If I looked like a mouse to Marian, scurrying this way and that to perform errands for the cats in my life, so be it.

By the next morning, I agreed to do as Astrid wished. Per's study was off limits; the archivist from the university was due in August. Once the cataloging was completed, there would be a room in the research library for Per's papers and books, and the room would be named for him. We had come to the stage in life, I understood, when places were named for us. Or rather for them, for Per and Marian.

After breakfast, Astrid and I approached Per's wardrobe, and soon we got into the swing of it. When I tired or grew cranky, Astrid would become even more cheerful and practical, and so on until we got to the last drawer. In it we found a fat manila envelope filled higgledy-piggledy with family pictures, the ones I'd sent to Per when he was away; photos of Astrid as she stood and walked, learned to ride a bike; of the house and the outbuildings, a record made as each improvement was completed. We squeezed our pennies to make improvements. His studio. My studio. A guesthouse where we anticipated that Astrid would one day stay with her husband and children. There was rarely anyone else around, so there were no snapshots of Astrid and me together, though Astrid took a few shots of me in the kitchen or the vegetable garden. Because she was a child and many feet shorter than I, the views were not flattering, but I sent them anyway to show Per that our daughter was learning to use a camera.

At the bottom of the drawer was a man's cashmere sweater, a V-neck, wrapped in tissue paper, never worn. Astrid removed the soft black garment from its nest and exclaimed at how expensive such a sweater must have been. It was miraculously uneaten by the moths that plagued our house.

The sweater was in Per's suitcase when he returned from a PEN conference in Eastern Europe. His father had died the previous year—not swiftly, as Per would—and we'd agreed that Per should extend his visit and spend a few weeks after the conference with his family in Stockholm. When I was unpacking and he lying on our bed telling me about his time in Sweden, I came upon the sweater.

"A little treat for myself," he said. "At the conference."

I wondered how he came to buy a sweater from a Parisian store in an Eastern European city.

"Marian was there," he said. "We went shopping. She shops wherever she goes."

"She's such a resourceful person," I said.

"She's extravagant and generous," he said. "It's her way. She's always broke, you know."

"That's Marian," I said.

"She persuaded me that I couldn't live without that particular black sweater. I didn't want to tell you. You worry so about money."

Astrid wanted a garment of her father's to keep. Per was indifferent to clothes, so the cashmere sweater was the best Astrid could hope for. As for me, I'd assumed a souvenir would appear from his closets and drawers but it didn't. Astrid and I washed out all the places where her father had kept his clothing. Per's wedding ring and watch we set aside.

The following week, the house felt empty without Astrid. The bags of Per's clothing stayed in the trunk of my car until I unloaded them at the thrift shop for the women's shelter.

My little magazine piece was now a thousand words. With each new draft, all those words illuminated the beginning of my life with Per. Each time I read it over, our early happiness was more vivid.

Per and I hadn't been isolated in the mountains; there were others there and they were part of our happiness. Aside from the photographer and his boyfriend, there was the postman and the blind couple who ran the grocery store in the village. And Marian, of course, who visited a few times and then left our lives, or so we thought. Each person I remembered was a particular part of the year we lived in the adobe house, and the year was itself a piece of our life together, not the most important piece or the best.

July passed. August came. When I had arranged and rearranged my thousand words, I sent them to the magazine. The editor liked my little excursion in time, as he called it.

In our vegetable garden, the squash prospered and the tomatoes had their usual troubles. I lost many of them. The failure mattered less because Per wasn't there to plan the next summer's strategies.

Old friends invited me to the Cape and I went, though the effort of wresting myself from our house was painful. Several times, I almost canceled. Once I started driving east to the ocean, I was fine. When I returned to Vermont, it was the third week in August. I knew what lay ahead of me. Winter had come before, bringing isolation and peace.

There was no forethought. Certainly no malice aforethought. But when Marian called to say she was relieved to be back east after a prolonged visit to New Mexico and how wonderful it was that she could come up for Labor Day weekend, I said that it wouldn't be possible for her to visit. I meant to tell her that I was sorry, that I'd miss her. After all, we'd been friends a long time. But in the rush of Marian's talk about how she'd been celebrated and honored in her home state and how really gorgeous though ruined the place was, my opportunity passed.

Here It Was, November

The major Marian Foster Todd archive was among the holdings of the New York Public Library, but when she was diagnosed with her terminal illness, Marian sold her few remaining papers to the famous archival center in Austin. As ever she was desperate for money. Marian made many appearances in that capacious Texas library. There were references to her in letters and diaries in Austin's Sexton, Lowell, Auden, Bishop, and Creeley collections, for she was more comfortable with poets than with fiction writers like herself. A letter from Salinger to a family friend quoted a line from one of Marian's first published stories, and a postcard from Olivia Manning to Ivy Compton-Burnett mentioned meeting Marian in London and finding her less beautiful and more intelligent than expected. Marian lived to be an old woman and she put her oar in literary waters at an early age. One of the photos I planned to use in my biography was of young slim Marian smiling arm in arm with old broad Willa Cather in front of the Plaza Hotel. Marian prized that photograph above all others, even the glamorous ones taken by Irving Penn for *Harper's Bazaar* two decades later.

My biography of Marian Foster Todd, the capstone of my career, was all but written. Five years before, early on in my research, I'd gone to Austin, not yet convinced that I could undertake such a life. Two biographies of Marian had been published in her lifetime, neither one successful or, understandably, thorough. Now I knew the type of chocolate she preferred and that she claimed to sleep well only on ironed, white sheets. All the separate bits of Marian Foster Todd were collected and assembled for those who would not read her letters and diaries, would not hear the voices of those who knew her, might not even read her stories. Through my biography, the woman who had lived and died would live and die again.

The present trip to Austin was my final sojourn in the familiar country of archival research. One document evaded me and I hoped to find a trace of it in Austin, a certain letter to Marian Foster Todd from her dear friend, Sandra da Rocha, the renowned poet who lived her long life in Pomfret, Vermont. The correspondence between them, though sparse on Sandra's side, was frank and intimate. Even Marian's affair with Sandra's husband didn't strain their affection. What snapped the spine of their friendship was Marian's habit of arranging to visit and canceling at the last moment. Meticulous and elaborate planning would drag on for months about when Marian might arrive, bringing what and staying for how long, but this didn't stop Marian from sending a telegram or, later in life, picking up the phone to cancel the visit, often on the very day she was expected. She did this to all her friends. Her favorite excuse was that she'd finally become involved with her work after an unbearable drought and couldn't possibly interrupt it. According to Marian's ethos, the excuse of work was sacred, but she never understood that there was at hand a causal relationship: Marian arranged elaborate and burdensome visits, then canceled them as a way to force herself into work anew.

When Marian canceled a visit a short month after Sandra's husband died, Sandra wrote a blistering message of farewell and the two friends never spoke again. I longed to find Sandra's actual letter and quote it directly rather than rely on Marian's account, but the original was missing. It was Marian's custom to preserve her correspondence, even the most painful documentation of lost friendship and love, but not this particular letter. The carbon copy it was Sandra's habit to keep of every letter she wrote, major and minor, was nowhere to be found. Her farewell to Marian—"inexcusable," Marian called it—was reported in Marian's journal, so it was possible to approximate the contents of the letter. Sandra's papers were in Boston and I'd trolled them thoroughly.

My previous books had taught me that the first loyalty of the biographer was to truth, not to feelings or reputation. Marian Foster Todd quarreled eventually with everyone who meant anything to her, supplying me with decades of grudges to narrate and tangled emotions to sort. One puzzlement was the failure of her sophisticated friends to understand that what Marian did to one she would in time do to all; each considered himself or herself the single exception to Marian's cancellations, disappearances, and inconvenient reappearances. Why had each not been prepared for the moment when Marian would act exactly like Marian? The answer lay partially in Marian's personal charm, partially in her talent for finding friends whose need for love and inclusion was almost as great as her own. Marian's childhood had been spent among people who fought constantly and bitterly; she felt safest when she was stirring things up for people she liked. The reenactment of abandonment revived her spirit.

Marian justified her manipulation of others, her ruthless need for fulfillment on her own terms, as living in the service of her art. But others have lived lives just as lonely, made love just as difficult for those brave enough to try, without self-aggrandizing justification.

In the libraries and archives where I'd spent my adult existence, one's personal life was meaningless; only books, documents, archives, and collections, only the cataloged, counted. The reading room in Austin was a favorite, a granite bunker built into the hill below the main tower. In the anteroom hung the oil portrait of the pale young woman whose parents created the library in her memory; the visitor paused, then got on with her work. Time took on another quality altogether in the reading room; there I moved from obscurity to darkness.

The biographies that made my reputation were of other, relatively minor figures in twentieth-century American letters. Long ago I left academia, the little world I knew best. I worked alone, independent of an institution, with sparse financial backing. Through uncompromising research and skillful telling, my books made the lives of my subjects crucial context for understanding twentieth-century American literature, or so the reviewers asserted. Academic journals treated my work with respect. The books won prizes. In this, my final effort, the stakes were considerably higher. If I succeeded, Marian's place as an important, even canonical, novelist would be secured. Though the biographer was always an ancillary figure, my name and Marian's would be coupled after my death in a lasting sisterhood.

For the biographer, the final clue to character lies in the yet unread—the scribbled note, the diary page, a notation in the margin of a draft—until the day when even the most devoted portraitist of the dead says, *Enough!* Working in the service of the dead, biographers quit their labors only when the sole remaining task is the impossible—resurrection.

The guesthouse I rented in Austin lay at the back of a large, pleasant lot canopied by ancient live oaks; the guesthouse had a miniature kitchen and laundry, as well as a holly hedge to screen it from the main house. My landlord on my previous visits to Austin was a professor of astronomy. He'd since gone to join his stars, and a young academic couple now owned the place.

I unpacked my wardrobe—one skirt, one pair of dress pants, one pair for daily work—and started a list: soy milk, coffee. Though I had acquaintances in Austin, I had no interest in alerting them to my presence. In the past my visits to archives were occasions for the eager continuation of a friendship—this one in London, that dear old soul in Cambridge. At the present moment, silence and loneliness were preferable; human warmth might have tempted me to confide.

How many times in my scholar's life had I forced strange rooms to welcome me and, however temporarily, to become my own? In the past five years, in search of Marian Foster Todd, I'd breached the solitude of rented rooms and borrowed apartments in England, Ireland, and France, in New Haven and in Troy. Day after day I'd waited for the doors to open, anxious to secure my customary seat, my little home, all in the name of research.

The end of my travels was New York, my rent-controlled and by no means small apartment on the Upper West Side. Once I left my native state, I didn't advertise my beginnings except to say, *Oh, the middle of the country,* on the rare occasions when anyone asked. As a biographer, I was expected to answer questions on the smallest detail of my subject's origins; in exchange I was granted immunity from curiosity.

Like Marian Foster Todd, I never married. Once I came close but I resisted. My fate lay elsewhere, I thought grandly. My family had dwindled over the years to a cousin I heard from at Christmas. My friends in New York were dear but I expected nothing from them.

In the guesthouse mirror, I looked at my present face for the past one and waited for the two to merge. The essence of a person stays intact from birth; I was the same as I was at eight when I checked in the mirror, trying to see myself as others saw me. But the body changes. When I looked at my hands now, I didn't see them clutching the handlebars as I pedaled along the streets of my riverbank village in my unnamed state. They looked like my father's hands, steady on the steering wheel of his Studebaker, resting across his chest in his coffin.

Marian left behind a string of male and female lovers, and Dorothea, her daughter. Dorothea's father was a handsome folksinger of no great talent who left before the birth of his child. In one of her last interviews, Marian said that she was brave until Dorothea was born, and then she knew, looking at the helpless baby, that she'd never write again if she stayed. She handed the infant over to a relative of the father's and promised never to communicate with the child. The crystalline moment of relinquishment reminded one of Marian's finest short stories.

When I phoned Dorothea from Austin, she spoke in her low warm voice of her plans for my visit—our Albuquerque mornings would begin with a walk through the nature center and a visit to the café I liked; we'd take a tram ride to the top of the mountain; her garden was prepared for my inspection, the sturdy desert plants eager to hear that I admired them. During this visit I hoped to sleep in the guest room where Marian had died. The bed was swaddled in white covers and pillows, placed so that Marian could view the passing day without having to raise her head. There, Marian suffered the end of her beauty and the final humiliations of her body. The room opened onto Dorothea's garden. The view was silver, lavender, and misty green against the blue adobe wall.

Dorothea and I had years of letters and phone calls between us as well as my two previous trips to New Mexico, the first to persuade her to reveal the story of herself and her mother, the second to show that I was sincere in my affection.

"Yes, yes, how wonderful, I can't wait," I said.

It didn't seem as though we'd have enough time—or I the stamina—to do all that she'd decided we must, but I hated to tell Dorothea how exhausted I was after a day doing nothing more strenuous than reading. Dorothea would have done anything for me. The careful work of not taking advantage of her was all mine.

In Dorothea, as in so much else, Marian Foster Todd was a lucky woman, and I shared some of her good fortune. Their separation and reunion bestowed shape on a life that might otherwise appear to be one capricious lurch followed by another, the only constant Marian's struggle to write.

With the fearsome diagnosis still fresh, Marian understood that she needed a place to die. She arranged to give a reading at the University of New Mexico and contrived to meet Dorothea and to inspect her house behind its blue adobe wall. Dorothea lived in New Mexico, unmarried, in her late forties, working at a clerical job with the goal of early retirement in the state system. Her adoptive parents were dead. She'd spent years nursing them through their final illnesses, one and then the other. Meeting Marian's high standards in every way, Dorothea found herself in possession of her long-lost and dying mother.

"You'll be here soon," Dorothea said.

"I might have to stay here in Austin longer. If I find anything new."

My warning, my hedge against Dorothea's greater energy, alarmed me, and I wondered if I'd gone too far. If everything went smoothly, Dorothea was fine, but *smoothly* meant no break to her routine. Life wasn't like that, not even a life as simple as Dorothea's.

When she was a child, Dorothea fell off her bike and a piece of gravel lodged in her cheek. It looked like a cunningly placed birthmark, but she considered herself disfigured. More beautiful than her famous mother, she allowed no photographs to be taken of her. Whereas Marian strived, even at her poorest, to dress strikingly, Dorothea wore ironed white button-downs over jeans in winter, white T-shirts over shorts in summer. On the third anniversary of Marian's death, her *Collected Stories* was published to great acclaim, and the Albuquerque newspaper assigned a reporter to a profile of Dorothea, sending her first into terror that she'd have to talk about herself, next into burning guilt that she'd let Marian down. In the end, Dorothea referred the reporter to me. "Do what you have to do," she said, her cheer restored, her anxiety lifted. "You always do." Dorothea's tone was fond and a little amused at my thoroughness, my hard labor that would benefit her more than it ever would me.

"Oh," Dorothea said. "We'll go to Acoma Pueblo. And the little church in Chimayó where the pilgrims leave their shoes.

"You'll love Acoma," she said. "It was where Willa Cather set her enchanted mesa. Marian told me."

It wasn't true that Cather had based her famous New Mexico story there. Dorothea didn't read, and Marian often misremembered.

In my apartment far away in New York, the radio played softly to discourage burglars, dust settled on every surface, and the black phone waited at attention for the call from the specialist, telling me he'd reached his diagnosis. Once given a name, my disease would take over and there would be little left to my life but the treatment protocol. Was it any wonder that I refused to check the messages waiting for me?

When Marian was on her way to what she called her last real disaster, she didn't wait for bad news but pursued it as aggressively as she ever had a man or publicity for her books or a teaching job to spare her another minute of living from hand to mouth. Her doctors, all of whom I'd interviewed, started out by admiring Marian. Only Dorothea had been patient enough to sustain her mother's leaving of the world. All human actions are self-serving; there must have been something appealing to Dorothea about sustaining Marian through her illness. Dorothea would have been within her rights to send her packing. Dorothea wouldn't discuss her decision with me, saying it was only natural for her to care for Marian: "Who else would take care of her?" Dorothea didn't know that someone else would have appeared, as someone always had for Marian.

Who would appear for me? When the phone call caught up

with me, when I heard the expected words, who would care for me when I was unable to care for myself? There was no Dorothea in my life to soften the mortal blow.

When I died someone would empty my apartment, and that someone would dispose of my small art collection, cabinets of papers, thousands of books. My jewelry was worthless. My clothes were hopeless. No vintage treasures hid in my closet, only the most utilitarian packables and washables. My only hope was that close to the end there would be a kind of friend to take on my leftovers, though I'd lived long enough to know that there would come a time when this wouldn't worry me any longer. My possessions, which I went through every year, subtracting and adding, would no longer be my concern.

In Austin, I swam in Barton Springs, and here it was, November. Fallen leaves on the water clung to me as I passed the lifeguard stations and the deserted diving board. Where the springs entered the pool, I pushed down into the water where the most beautiful colors waited and I imagined that death would be like this but without the effort. Then I struggled up to the surface, gasping for air. My body, it seemed, wanted to live. When I showered in the bathhouse, I found clumps of algae and leaves stuck to my body. I might have pressed down to feel the tumor. It would do no harm. My doctor had shown me the method and demonstrated the correct pressure to use. Still, I felt no desire to know its shape or to probe its private life.

Once you've done biographical research, once you've written a life, you understand the obvious, that you don't know anyone else. You can't. Now I knew the answer to the sophomoric question *Is it possible to know one's self?* The disease was my biography. Soon enough it would expose my life's secrets to me, its only reader.

* * *

The table I claimed as my little home was at the back of the reading room. While I squinted at a barely legible note from a once-famous professor approaching Marian to teach at his university (an event that never transpired), I became aware that someone stood at my side, a shaven-haired youth, barely a man. He wore the ill-fitting cotton jacket of a reading-room runner, and he spoke my name in a hushed tone.

It occurred to me that my doctor was more resourceful than I'd imagined and that the news had reached me even here. I shivered, suddenly aware of how cold the room was. The boy swiveled to reveal that he held a box with a call slip stuck in it.

Across the elegant room, past the other scholars bent over papers, books, and small computers, the reading-room supervisor, an amiable woman who bred corgis, was waving to me. On a previous visit, I visited a litter of newborn corgi puppies and considered taking one back to New York with me, a ridiculous idea. She was smiling; she'd sent the runner over and was watching for my reaction. I waved back, pantomiming surprise and delight.

To be present when new material was released to public examination was nothing short of a sign, and I paused to consider Marian's orchestration. The present moment—the release of the box to public scrutiny—was exactly seven years from the date of Marian's death in Albuquerque. According to the terms of her will, all of her other papers were made available immediately upon her death; only the box before me had been forbidden. Familiar as I was with the ins and outs of Marian's decisions, I hadn't even been aware of the existence of new material.

Three letters in white envelopes and a spiral-bound notebook. Marian carried such notebooks with her to compose stories, but she was just as likely to use the pages for grocery lists, for inventories of her wardrobe, or as a diary for recording daily events. Her formal journals were hand-bound, an annual gift from an old friend in London even after they ceased to speak.

There, in the notebook, in Marian's beautiful hand, was something like a love story, set in New Mexico, time period undefined. A month after a kind of troubadour and a lovely young girl meet, they marry against the wishes of her family. He takes her to his ancestral home, a once magnificent adobe on the edge of town. There they live alone.

They enjoy one month of happiness.

One night the husband tells his bride that he must leave. She says that she'll go with him. He insists that she stay. She must trust him. He has his reasons for not explaining. She awakens alone to the sounds of morning in the large house, then hears an unfamiliar noise, a repeated shrill cry. She decides that it's an animal trapped in one of the empty rooms. In her long nightgown, she wanders, trying to locate the source of the sound. Eventually, she opens the door of a room on the opposite side of the courtyard. There she finds a baby, perhaps six months old, in a wooden cradle that's rocking from side to side as the infant kicks and waves its arms. The baby is frantic and, as the bride discovers when she lifts the child, wet, soiled, and hungry.

At this point, the story changes, no longer a melodrama but a more familiar Marian Foster Todd tale.

In time the bride discovers that her husband has another wife who bore their daughter and abandoned her, disappearing to parts unknown. Now that the baby's father is gone also, the discarded bride is left to care for the helpless, fragile, needy infant. The bride stands over the infant, knowing that if she accepts being the baby's mother, her life will be over at seventeen.

The ending is ambiguous and the possibilities terrible, an obvious homage to Chekhov's well-known "Sleepy," in which the overburdened servant, herself a child, strangles the baby in her care to get some peace. Murder isn't beyond the implications of Marian's story, the metaphorical death of the child bride or the actual death of the baby.

Though there was more to read, I closed the notebook, returned it to the box, and left the reading room, signaling to the room supervisor that I'd be back. It was lunchtime, and I wandered down the hill to the new computer sciences building. The café was crowded with faculty and students. I found a small table far away from the suspended television set with its mute display of news. My heart pounded. Adrenaline narrowed my throat.

The strength of Marian's work derived from her clear vision of the lives of her characters; it was impossible to say which she favored, for she created them with a cold impartial hand. The story in the notebook read more like a message than a work of fiction, but it was a message in a language I didn't know.

The midday sun and my heart's painful rhythm made my trek up to the reading room as difficult as scaling a mountain.

There were a few blank pages in the notebook; Marian often reserved space for later amendments before beginning another story. The second was in a more familiar style.

An affair set in New Mexico, between a professional singer who's down on his luck and a young girl disillusioned about love because of an earlier betrayal. She hopes that now she's found a truthful lover. The girl leaves her family and moves into his rented adobe at the edge of town. They enjoy a month of careful happiness, and she begins to trust him. One night he announces that he has to get out of town. She'll go with him, the girl says. He declares that he must travel alone. They quarrel bitterly, and she accuses him of planning from the start to leave her. When she wakes up the next morning, he and his few possessions are gone. In a skilled passage, the girl realizes how little he had with him and how easy his exit was. Hearing a noise from the next room, she hopes that he's returned, but instead there's a baby in a wooden cradle, crying and, the girl finds, wet and soiled.

At first reluctantly, the girl cares for the baby. She begins to find meaning in her daily tasks and to feel a kind of love. After a few weeks, the baby's aunt and uncle appear. The uncle, a lawyer, explains that the baby's mother, addled by drugs, left the infant there with the father. Since he's gone too, they intend to raise the baby as their own. At that moment, the girl realizes that in this affair, she is not the heroine and has no rights at all.

The end is the best part: the girl's sorrow at losing the baby; her simultaneous recognition that she's had a narrow escape.

The second tale was more naturalistic, also less touching than the more sentimental and heightened version. In no way was I overcome by my reading.

My back was giving its familiar library twinges. Closing the notebook, keeping its contents from prying eyes, I strolled past the portrait of the donors' daughter. Crowded on top of the card catalogs were bronze busts of writers and poets whose papers rested in the collection. None, not even the most egomaniacal, would welcome a biographer; they were too smart for that. I inspected their well-known faces, some ordinary, some grotesque, some beautiful. Their disapproval rained down on me. When I embarked on the biography, I was convinced that Marian's was a story worth telling. Her reputation in the years following her death took a dive, as always happens, but by the time the book was finished, I calculated, it would be the moment for a reappraisal of the work. But what of Marian's privacy? What gave me the right to know her secrets?

The third story was a first-person narration in the confessional tone Marian perfected in her most anthologized tale.

The narrator is a young woman, no longer a girl but much younger than her lover, a journalist from Los Angeles who's in her small town in New Mexico for an extended rest. He's just dried out and needs to be in a simple, cheap place in order to stay away from drink. The young woman is a fairly straightforward version of Marian at that age, with only geography and physical features changed here and there. She's the brightest young woman in town, discontent with her opportunities, without the means or momentum to leave. The man, even though he's a drunk and a has-been, represents her chance for a new life. His reluctance to become involved with her, given his age and condition, is conveyed with subtlety and sympathy so that when he does fall in love, the reader is moved. It is guaranteed that something terrible will happen. In Marian's stories, love is always prelude to disaster.

In the story's second act, the narrator shows her lover, for lovers they become, the beauty of her birthplace, which, in her discontent and restlessness, she has stopped seeing. He tells her stories of a larger, city life, the one they intend to lead together.

And then. The fatal *and then,* the turning of the worm, the curve in the road with only darkness ahead.

And then one day, the narrator awakens to find her lover packing. There was a phone call in the middle of the night but he assured her that it was a drunken friend. Now he tells her that he has to leave. He'll send for her as soon as he's settled. *But where will you go?* she asks. *How will I reach you?* He doesn't know. *I'll go with you.* He won't let her. He'll write. He promises.

The appearance of the word *promise* in Marian's work is another sign of doom.

The man leaves, and the woman is left to face the town alone; all the old biddies pronounce her used and abandoned. The man has paid for the house for the rest of the month, so she stays there, taking long walks and trying to decide what to do next: Go to Los Angeles to find her lover? Wait patiently for his return? Travel east to a different destiny? One afternoon she returns from a walk and hears a strange noise. In the living room, a baby in a wooden cradle, kicking and crying. When she lifts the baby she finds that it's wet and soiled.

She contacts a favorite cousin, a nurse at a nearby hospital, and together they care for the baby until a letter arrives from the man. The baby was born six months before; he's the father, and his wife, hitherto unmentioned, is the mother. The wife is an alcoholic who left their infant daughter at the address she had for him, the rented adobe in New Mexico. Now the wife is gone, and the lover plans to disappear. The baby is the girl's to keep. But she doesn't keep it. She persuades her cousin, who's older, married, and unhappily child-less, to take the baby, and she gets on a bus headed east. The story ends with a lyrical description of the desert between New Mexico and Texas.

It is problematic to seek in literature—drafts or finished work—the facts of a writer's life. It took nothing from Marian's skill to say that she used her life in all her work, to assert that there was nowhere in her fiction an example of an event wholly invented. In my nearly completed book, I resisted the temptation to use the life as a map to the work or the work as a map to the life, but now I read the stories in the notebook with the iciness one feels on hearing confirmed a dreadful truth one has suspected unconsciously.

Often I wished that Marian had acted more nobly in her personal relationships, but nothing she did sickened me until she sought out Dorothea and persuaded her daughter to see her through her last days. Marian's final act was the one I'd struggled with, trying to maintain moral neutrality so that I could report the facts, leaving judgment to others.

Once I met Dorothea, I became almost reconciled to Marian's late-life claiming of her daughter. However self-serving it was of Marian, however calculated to gain a safe nest and a devoted nurse while she was dying, for Dorothea the reunion with her birth mother and the chance to care for her was the fulfillment of a life's wish. Before Marian, Dorothea had been troubled and lonely, without a sense of her place in the world, and she attributed this, despite her love for her adoptive parents and theirs for her, to her missing mother. She was nearly a recluse, working by day at a state office job, returning to her much-loved house and garden in the evening. Her parents had been her closest friends and now they were gone. Her dogs, her garden, occasional forays to the Four Cor-ners or nearby pueblos: These made up Dorothea's quiet life. She confessed to me that, before Marian, she fretted that she didn't do enough either in or for the world. But then Marian appeared, and Dorothea's life suddenly had meaning; she became Marian Foster Todd's daughter, her loving nurse, and, finally, her grateful heir. Dorothea's debt to the world was paid and her place in it secured.

Work dominated Marian's life, her process of procrastination and avoidance followed by total relinquishment to the work, and her constant struggle to meet her own high standards and her idea of herself. In the end, though, Marian's art was not enough. Marian had outlived many of her friends and all of her friendships. She hated her few living relatives. Seeking out Dorothea, finding her worthy, causing dramatic havoc in her daughter's life, appealed to Marian and gave the degradation of her illness and death a pleasing narrative shape.

It didn't seem so terrible. Awaiting my own bad news, I envied Marian. At the end of Marian's life, when she needed a daughter, she inserted herself into Dorothea's life, pushing aside the couple, now dead, who had nurtured Dorothea, replacing them with her glorious if dying self. Still, my biographer's abhorrence of literal congruence between life and work didn't mean that I couldn't connect the dots. In the cool, concentrated air of the reading room, my sad confidence grew that Marian was not Dorothea's mother. The stories in the notebook would break Dorothea's heart.

It was closing time. I put away the notebook and carried the box to the desk, leaving it on the cart where it would wait for me until morning.

That evening as I unlocked the guesthouse, my landlady, a specialist in French medieval market practices, rushed from the kitchen of the main house saying, "I didn't want to leave a note." Her denim apron protected a festive shirt from the local Indian store.

If a message is meant to get through, it will. I believed that the doctor in New York had phoned this young woman.

She said, "You must come to our party tonight." A cocktail

party: a candidate for a chair and the spouse whom the psychology department would have to take on before the deal was sealed.

"Oh, my dear," I said. "I've had a trying day and a party's the last thing . . ."

As so often in my life, the other shoe dropped. She was inviting me pro forma so that the inevitable noise would have to be excused.

"But I'll try," I said, and her face brightened. "I'll have a rest, and I'll try."

The truth was, I couldn't bear to speak to anyone.

After a shower and a bite to eat, I retreated to the tiny patio, where I wouldn't be seen by the partygoers. It was a pleasant night, warm for November. That morning I'd had a swim but the muscles in my arms ached and my back complained after the day in the reading room. Perhaps it was not simple muscle fatigue but a harbinger of what was to come. The sound of laughter and the murmur of lecturing that passed for academic conversation formed the background to my thoughts.

If Dorothea was not Marian's daughter but the abandoned child of a former lover and his wife, then Dorothea represented not Marian's late-life acceptance of the deepest connection of all, but another connivance on Marian's part.

The story Marian had confessed to a few close friends about looking at her baby and realizing that she'd never live the life she wanted if she gave in to her maternal instincts—that was true. The twist, the turn, was that the baby she relinquished was not her own.

My discovery destroyed the heartwarming shape of my book. So often in my research it seemed that Marian was a force rather than a human being, and that her own survival was all that mattered to her. To show her as a mother at the end of her life, to be able to say that she loved someone else—loved Dorothea, her daughter—gave Marian a missing dimension of humanity. Now, in the light of my new findings, if I bought Marian's version of her motherhood, I'd be a sentimental fool. If I didn't, if I revealed the new material and proved my case as best I could, all received ideas of Marian's character would have to be altered. No longer would Marian seem a relic of the past; her ruthlessness would mark her as a truly contemporary figure, and the sensational revelation would be the making of my biography.

Beyond my literary calculations lay the horror of what the revelation would do to Dorothea: to gain a mother out of nowhere, to nurse her and learn to love her, then Marian's death, then to learn that she had been duped—Dorothea would be destroyed, though, as Marian once remarked, "People are so rarely destroyed."

By this time, the party was ending: early classes, babysitters, the stranglehold and welcome embrace of domestic and academic routine. The night was over for me too, and I picked up my wineglass and went inside.

As I washed the dishes and arranged my papers for the next day's work, I realized that, though I'd searched the official records and all of Marian's papers, there might be other evidence and living witnesses I'd missed. Marian might have planted such bombs in archives all over the country. Her carefully timed revelation, the new box released seven years after her death, might be only the first of many that one by one would diminish the worth of all I averred.

Little by little, my achievement, my life's work, might be discounted until it sat unread on library shelves, remaindered in bookstores, unwanted at any price.

On all three letters in the box, Marian's name and address were written at the top in blue ballpoint in block letters. There was no return address. Two of the letters were nearly fifty years old, addressed to Marian at the boardinghouse in the Village where she'd lived on her first arrival in New York.

The first was brief:

Tinky told me what you did with the baby. It wouldn't be any use to ask what you thought you were doing. But I'll be a fool and ask. Couldn't you stand to wait for me?

I'd never seen the name *Tinky* before. The letter was signed with only a letter: *B.*

The second letter was longer. It began with a Whitmanesque celebration of names of all the places B had been since he left Marian and the baby, then turned into a catalog of hard jobs he'd taken and his chances for good fortune that turned bad, and then:

You like to hear the end of stories. My baby's mother is dead. They won't even let me see my baby. The so-called mother swears she'll fight me to the death. She has the money to hire a lawyer and you know me. Your words of love meant nothing and your promises less. You were my last chance and you knew it.

B had managed to enrage her or at least to touch a sore spot; she must have replied to the first letter. If I'd received any of Marian's scathing prose, I'd have crumbled on the spot, but B evidently enjoyed infuriating her. He reminded her of their plans to raise the child and then said:

Anyone would think you cared about the baby. Or me. You called her your own. I never figured you for a natural but you looked like for once you cared for someone other than yourself. That's why I trusted you with my baby girl.

The third letter was much more recent, addressed to Marian at her last New York residence. Two years before her diagnosis and the onset of the disease's symptoms, Marian signed a lease on a floor-through in the Village. The beautiful apartment was meant to be the place where she would be a famous and successful author, at home at last. It had been decades since Marian had had a place of her own. She'd traveled in Europe and Latin America, perched in San Francisco and Chicago, and of course found temporary shelters during her many stints as a visiting professor. For years, she'd called herself a cuckoo bird, I thought in reference to her habit of living in other people's houses, though now an additional meaning came clear: Some cuckoos lay their eggs in other nests and leave their young to be raised by other birds.

Marian's last apartment had white walls and pale furniture, polished floors and soft rugs. Vases of flowers everywhere. She must have stood many times at the front window, where her view was of the redbrick, three-story houses across the street, window boxes filled with geraniums and lobelias. She'd described doing just that in letters. The oblique angle of observation appears in her penultimate story, "Enfilade," when the main character is shocked to see her former lover walking past, he unaware that she stands watching him. Once again, Marian was a step ahead of me; I'd assumed that the story's vivid moment was inspired by nothing more than the view from her front room.

His last letter was brief:

No thanks to you no thanks to me the baby's grown to be a fine woman right where you left her. Not a day goes by that I don't curse you for taking her from me.

If B's letters were to be believed, he'd entrusted his baby to Marian, who'd relinquished her and fled. Marian wasn't Dorothea's mother. B's third letter came at the first moment that she needed a daughter. She arranged the reading at the University of New Mexico at half her usual fee, inspected Dorothea, and saved herself. Throughout my years of research, I'd wondered off and on how Marian knew that Dorothea was still in Albuquerque, but I'd figured she was just lucky.

The stories in Marian's notebook would make an intriguing appendix to my book. The lover was not a stock Marian male; he was a drunk and she had no use for alcoholic men in her art. Babies appear only twice in Marian's work, but in those instances are adorable and savvy in a comical way. In none of the three versions of what I now called the Austin story was the baby appealing—not appealing enough for Marian to fight for, not appealing enough to keep.

Add the three stories to Marian's statements to interviewers about her moment of temptation before she abandoned Dorothea—so congruent with the drafts in the notebook—add the fact that she had reserved the notebook and letters until she knew she would be dead, and I had the possibility of coming as close to the truth as Marian would permit.

Nothing could stop me from publishing my new finds: Early on, Dorothea had signed a form giving me access to all of her mother's papers and permission for me to photocopy and publish whatever I wished. No one could have been more generous than she. Her signature on the permission form, and on all the notes and cards she'd sent me over the years, was rounded, childish, loving.

In the chill of the reading room, I had a moment of the sort of rare understanding that illuminates Marian's stories. The content of the letter I'd hoped to find in Austin—the farewell from Marian's dearest friend—was now obvious.

Sandra, the poet, alone of Marian's large circle, must have known Marian's secret. The entry in the poet's journal at the end of the friendship declared that Marian was incapable of love. The missing letter must have specifically condemned Marian for abandoning the baby entrusted to her, the infant who became Dorothea. Marian destroyed the original. Sandra must have destroyed her carbon copy out of a loyalty to Marian that endured even after she couldn't bear to be with her, and Sandra's loyalty held fast even after Marian so outrageously claimed Dorothea for her own.

B was Brandon Miller. Best remembered as the model for a heroic figure in Beat literature and lore, Brandon Miller was an action painter of unfulfilled promise. He was an alcoholic. They had been lovers when both were young and poor, before each moved to New York; by coincidence both were living in Greenwich Village, blocks apart, in old age, at the time of Marian's diagnosis. They had no contact, so far as I could tell from my exhaustive examination of Marian's date books, journals, and letters. Brandon Miller outlived Marian. Only a year ago, he died in the town where he was born, near Mt. Shasta in Northern California. In Miller's obituary in the *Times,* his liaison with Marian was mentioned, hers one name on a list.

When I last lunched with my editor in New York, she mentioned that a young writer, someone I'd recommended for a Guggenheim, was shopping around a proposal for a biography of Brandon Miller. When my fellow biographer came to Austin, as he would without question, and read the contents of the box, Brandon Miller's fatherhood of Marian's abandoned baby would make a juicy chapter. Still, no matter how Brandon Miller's biographer hurried, my book would be finished before his. The opportunity was mine to reveal Marian's dearest secret.

Now, my book might cause the kind of stir that mere dogged research wouldn't, for I could unveil Marian as a fraud, right up to her last day on earth. Never a fraud in her writing, often in her life. The new material offered something better than a happy ending. Marian, on the cusp of obscurity, would be newly famous as the selfish and brilliant charmer she was in life. All her fiction would be brought back into print, and the young—some of them—who knew her name vaguely, her work even less well, would discover her as a lifelong rebel and a devoted artist.

If my book succeeded, I would hold briefly what the world had to offer—modest fame for what remained of my lifetime; my book in all the bookstores and libraries; and, most elusive and unquantifiable, readers. My book would be something to leave behind, aside from my apartment filled with worn possessions of no great value to anyone, not even myself.

I repacked the letters and the notebook in their acid-free box and, saying grateful farewells to the reading room staff, I left a request for a copy of the notebook and letters to be sent to me in New York.

November was half over. Winter would come even here. That morning, I'd felt a chill in the air and decided to swim in the evening. Now I had the energy only to walk through the dusty autumn streets back to the guesthouse.

My flight to Albuquerque was early in the morning so I packed that night. As usual after a bout of research, I had more papers than ever. My clothing returned to its place in the suitcase obediently. In no time, I removed all trace of the small rearrangements that had made the guesthouse my home. When I'd changed into my night-dress and performed my nocturnal libations, I lay in bed, overcome by an exhaustion irreparable by sleep.

Dorothea lived in a modest neighborhood in the north valley of Albuquerque. Her house was hidden from the street by a high adobe wall, a blue that was fading with age into the most delicate shade of white. In back of the house, Dorothea tended a vegetable patch and an orchard. Small crisp pears came in autumn; apricots ripened in July. Her dogs patrolled the garden paths and used afternoons on the back porch to guard the world. Butterflies visited Dorothea's garden, and birds of all kinds. Though you heard cars pass, dogs bark, music from neighbors, it felt as though you were far from the rest of the world. Inside Dorothea's house, the tile floor was cool. The blades of the ceiling fans rotated sedately. Only there would it be possible for me to rest.

Here was food for thought, thoughts for the night ahead.

The Blue Wall

After Mother's death, Dorothea's friends from work took her out for happy-hour margaritas. Bright bougainvillea climbed the walls of the restaurant garden, and a big white umbrella shaded the women from the evening sun. Dolly and Tina said now that both her parents were gone, bless their souls, Dorothea could start living her own life. She could get rid of Mother's white Scottie and Daddy's black mutt. She'd been a good daughter. She had done everything for them. Dorothea was still young, no, no, she was. She still had a chance. Leave Albuquerque. Go to Europe. Go to South America. Take a chance, *mujer!* There was a world beyond this world. And love could come at any time to anyone. Women had healthy first babies in their forties, yes, it was true. Even that miracle might be waiting for Dorothea.

The old dogs greeted Dorothea's every appearance as if they'd been apart an eternity.

She'd always lived her own life. Who else's?

In the beauty of autumn, her favorite season, daily life was the tide that pulled Dorothea down and up again. She went to work, and on weekends she emptied drawers and closets, just as she had when her father died. Mother's clothing went to the poor, except for one of the linen shirts she'd sewn for herself and Dorothea. When Dorothea was a child, strangers remarked that mother and daughter looked so much alike, which made Mother laugh. Dorothea ripped threadbare towels and sheets, created a mountain of rags, put the rags in a box and the box in the garage. She went through the oak desk in the hall where Mother had sat every month to pay the bills, and destroyed a lifetime of income-tax returns and canceled checks, marveling that so much had been done with so little money. A yellowed file, *Dorothea Adoption,* held no clue to the identity of her birth parents. Her birth certificate and adoption papers were in the original envelope from the lawyer in Mother's hometown in Texas; Dorothea's birthplace was given as Santa Fe, New Mexico, Mother and Daddy as her parents.

She put the file in a box with her insurance papers, bankbook, and copies of her parents' will and death certificates. Daddy's illness, when Dorothea moved back home, had lasted six months. Mother had died less than a year later. It had been only so many months and days, but losing them both made the time feel longer.

That winter, Dorothea joined a group of knitters and crocheters, all women. The monthly meetings rotated from house to house; a founding principle was that no one would go to any fuss. They found a glass of wine, some food, a place to sit, and took out their work. One person spoke, then another. One woman told a story or remembered a time from another life, they laughed in high discordant notes, and Dorothea understood why women were accused of witchcraft.

Some in the group were talented; others, like herself, wielded hook or needle as a courtesy. She chose crochet, beginning a white cover for her bed. Compared to the warring of knitting needles, the tango of hook and thread was amiable. At first, she only crocheted with the group, then took it up at dusk, her hands accomplishing what her eyes couldn't see. Carolina, a soft-voiced woman who crocheted baby blankets for a store in Old Town, offered to teach Dorothea how to make a rug out of the rags from Mother's house.

Joe Martinez, a realtor friend of her father's, recommended that she wait until spring to put the house on the market. He was a tall man who smiled seldom as they looked at houses. Dorothea wanted to be in the north valley; along with the established farms and vineyards, there were old and new adobes, modest brick-faced ranch houses, shacks of one sort and another, but none was right.

Toward the end of winter, one of the knitters, Ellen, mentioned Pueblo Luna between Osuna and Second, a shortcut she took mornings on her way to her bookstore. Some of the houses on the block were iffy, some were fixed up. A For Sale sign had just appeared.

Two rectangular concrete-block buildings faced each other: The larger one, closer to the street, was a workshop; the smaller was a storage and tool shed. At the end of the alley formed by the buildings was a leafless pear tree; beyond it, a tangle of brush and cactus. An acre of mess, said Mr. Martinez, but a crew could cut everything down.

"Pueblo Looney," said Tina and Dolly after they drove past the place. "Isn't life hard enough?"

Dorothea worried that she wouldn't get the place, then that she would.

"That's the nature of desire," said Sally, the oldest of the knitters. "It twists you."

In early spring, her parents' house sold quickly. What she wanted to keep went into storage: furniture and books; watercolors and oils of adobes, cacti, bluebonnets, and mountains; family photographs, dishes, and glasses. After the closing, Dorothea drove straight to Pueblo Luna.

Every blade of grass, every weed, every broken window and warped door was hers alone.

The Saturday after the closing, Carolina's husband Manuel appeared with two cousins. The old dogs went crazy, then retreated to the shade.

By the end of the weekend, both buildings were empty. At the curb was a mountain of wood and glass, twigs, branches, bags of dead leaves. "I dislike giving advice," Manuel said, "but you need a wall. All the way around." Manuel's uncle Rico was a mason. He could build a concrete-block wall and cover it with stucco. He could build anything.

Dorothea camped out in the smaller building, and the dogs slept beside her. At dawn, a rooster woke her, then came the low intimate sound of horses nickering where ramshackle barns and stables backed up to the irrigation ditch.

In the city where she'd lived all her life a new world appeared: plumbing fixtures and old Mexican doors, ceramic tiles and wooden flooring, debarked vigas, dented appliances, and the people who sold these things and had been doing so all along. The smaller building became her bedroom and bath. Double doors opened to a walled garden. The larger building faced the mountains; it held the kitchen, living room, dining room, a second bedroom and bathroom. Each house had its own portale. The new wall curved like an egg, cutting off the corners of the lot. She chose the third shade of blue Rico offered for the stucco, the one that turned violet in certain sunsets.

Rico's brother-in-law, the cabinetmaker, built curved wooden gates, one at the street, the other past the pear tree to the vegetable garden, which Rico fenced with hog wire. When the deep, covered portales were finished, the two buildings were closer together.

In the fall, the women came to Pueblo Luna. They brought wine and fruit juice and ceramic bowls full of food. Sally tripped on a rug and spilled champagne: "Now the house is baptized." They ate and drank, and they approved of the work that had been done so far, Dorothea's plans for the future, and the way Dorothea had arranged the family furniture. At the end of the evening, as everyone was winding up cotton and wool and silk, one of the knitters, Ellen, said, "A place like this . . . You're inviting . . . *episodes,* Dorothea. I know it."

Dorothea doled out her money carefully. Dolly and Tina warned her about the unscrupulousness of the trades, but Dorothea wasn't stolen from or cheated. The only person who made a serious mistake was Rico's nephew, just out of rehab, and he redid the tile he'd laid in the second bathroom. The perennials and herbs matured. She cultivated the vegetable garden, and the dogs protected it from rabbits. Apricots and pomegranates grew easily.

For the second time the voice came out of the silence.

"Are you there? Have I reached Dorothea Browne?"

"Yes, ma'am."

"For a week or so. At the university. In residence, as they call it. And for a reading of my work—I write, you see. Well, maybe you don't. The reason for my call, so out of the blue—I knew your mother. A very long time ago. When you were born—"

"Ma'am. Mother's died."

"Oh, I know all about that. This is awkward, isn't it, darling? The point is—May I take you to dinner? Tomorrow? They've given me my own car, I told them I had to have some means of getting around. I could come to your house, pick you up." The woman stopped, and when she spoke again the voice was soft. "I know so few people at this juncture. Here in Albuquerque."

Dorothea gave the woman directions to the house on Pueblo Luna. It was May, evening, after work. Mother had never mentioned anyone named Marian Foster Todd.

There was a notice in the *Albuquerque Express* about the reading at the university, and *Life/Style* ran an interview with Marian Foster Todd and a photograph. She was delicate featured, like Mother, like Dorothea, but beautiful, with a rosebud mouth and pale indications of eyebrows. She was probably in her seventies or even her early eighties; Marian Foster Todd declined to give the interviewer an exact number, saying she'd changed her mind about her age so many times she couldn't possibly remember the truth. Her white hair was gathered in a loose knot at the base of her neck. Nothing about the woman was accidental.

A black car pulled in the gravel driveway. The dogs, who'd been sleeping, stretched and barked. A small woman in a tweed suit with an old-fashioned walking skirt emerged. She looked back at the street, then at Dorothea, at the curved wooden gate and the dogs panting at her feet.

"It's me, dear," Marian said.

Dorothea opened the gate. The woman retrieved her alligator handbag and locked the car. Her gaze met Dorothea's and she laughed.

"That must look so ungracious. I'm a New Yorker now. After all these years. Though I'm a native. From here, you know."

Marian balanced on her high heels along the stone path. Two glasses and a pitcher of iced tea waited by the chairs in the shade of the big building's portale.

"How inviting. Your own small world behind your blue wall, your house and a casita—in the Mexican fashion. May I have a tour at once? Before we settle into a good talk."

Marian was enchanted and she grew more delighted when she entered the small building and saw, past the bed, the garden of scented perennials and herbs. She admired the oak bedstead from Mother's family and the white cover Dorothea had crocheted.

"I live alone too," Marian said when they settled with their glasses of tea. "In Greenwich Village. At last I have the perfect place, a floor-through—white walls everywhere, and polished floors. I have three pieces of furniture that are really good, and I had them reupholstered in pale shades. Soft rugs. And I have enough money to keep vases of fresh flowers everywhere. Across the street, the houses are three stories, old, brick with window boxes filled with geraniums and lobelias in the summer months—that striking red and blue against the brick walls. Have you been to New York?"

"I knew people in college who wanted to go."

"And did they?"

"We lost touch. Maybe they did."

"It's the great ritual in American life, moving to New York City. I've lived all over—Paris, London, small places too all over—but I return to New York. It doesn't feel like home but it's something else just as important."

"I've always lived in Albuquerque," Dorothea said.

"That was the life I expected to live," Marian said. "But things change in a long life. You never know what might happen—horror or ecstasy."

Dorothea said, "I haven't found much of either."

Marian sipped her tea.

"Your delightful garden isn't visible from here."

"My bedroom faces the garden. Away from the rest."

"You'd really have to go to some lengths to see into the bedroom from the street, wouldn't you? Quite protected. The garden wall and the blue wall."

Before they left for dinner, Dorothea asked, "Where did you say you knew Mother from?"

"She and I . . . your mother and someone I once knew were related, cousins, second or third. I was never that interested in family when I was young and the ones who could have told me every detail were still alive. I never got it straight in the way you never really get such things straight. When you're young, you don't care."

Dorothea put their glasses and the pitcher on a tray to carry to the kitchen.

Marian said, "Dorothea. What an old-fashioned name."

"It's a family name. From sisters named Althea and Dorothy. They're Texas names. From Mother's family."

Marian insisted that Dorothea drive the black car to the restaurant. Marian had a cocktail and they shared a bottle of wine. The food was simple and complicated, full of tastes new to Dorothea. Over coffee, Marian asked if Dorothea wouldn't drive her back to the hotel and keep the car—she didn't want to go anywhere without her.

Driving the big car home, greeting the dogs, readying herself for bed, Dorothea heard Marian talking, talking, talking. Dorothea fell asleep with the sound of Marian's voice still in her ears.

Dorothea took time off from work that week. Though Marian said she wanted more than anything to see Santa Fe again and to show her special places to Dorothea, she found a daily reason not to—the sky was threatening, she was eager to know if a certain shop was still open in Albuquerque, there was a view she wanted to show Dorothea west of town. In the end, there was no time for Santa Fe. Marian confided words she'd never uttered to another soul so that Dorothea would know everything, good and bad, and Marian would have someone to know her at last. She talked about her travels; the ins and outs of her career; a green sweater she'd left in a Paris taxi in the sixties; illnesses that had come, threatened, and gone. She talked about flowers she loved and her favorite time of day. One morning over coffee she asked about the mark on Dorothea's cheek. Dorothea had fallen off her bike when she was eight. When she landed, a rock lodged in her cheek. The mark looked just like a blue star, Mother said, and though Daddy said the tiny rock would work its way out in time, it hadn't. Dorothea formed the habit of holding her hand over her cheek.

"You mustn't be ashamed. Without it, your face would be banal," Marian said.

Marian taught two classes and met with the officials from the university and a few professors, though she refused to attend either the cocktail party before her reading or the dinner afterward; she apologized to her hosts, but it was her well-established custom to be quiet before and after exposing her work to the public. The next day, she would fly back to New York.

The evening of the reading, Dorothea waited in the car outside the hotel. After twenty minutes, she went up to the room where Marian was "in the throes of indecision," torn between a black cocktail dress with a nipped waist and full skirt, very New Look, and a more contemporary Italian jacket, black, padded shoulders, and stovepipe trousers of the same moiré. Dorothea suggested the jacket and pants. Marian scorned the idea. Her audience expected her to look like a lady.

At last, they were out of the hotel and in the car, but Marian had to have a certain cherry cough drop, else her throat would go dry. As they drove from drugstore to grocery store to 7-Eleven, Dorothea couldn't help saying, "I hate keeping people waiting."

"Worry less about other people's convenience and more about your own. For God's sake, Dorothea, start taking better care of yourself."

A man in a suit and tie waited at the auditorium door. After he shook Marian's hand and she introduced him to Dorothea, he led her away, leaving Dorothea alone at the entrance.

The story Marian read was set in the mountains around Santa Fe. It began with a man and woman declaring undying love. When he abandoned her at the end of the story, the woman was nearly destroyed but resolved to live well without him and to remember always how it felt to be loved. The story's people and setting felt familiar to Dorothea though she'd never known them and the place seemed different.

When she was finished reading, Marian lowered her head. There was a second of silence, then a blast of applause.

Marian's admirers crowded around her, holding books to be signed, wanting to shake her hand or to say a few words of thanks for her stories. At last, Marian spotted Dorothea and gave a nod that Dorothea was sure no one else could detect. In the hotel, Marian ordered cognac from room service and talked for another hour.

Now Marian was gone with no plans to return. "Come to me," she told Dorothea at the airport. "Come to me."

Dorothea waited weeks to tell the knitting group about Marian Foster Todd's visit.

Of course they'd heard of Marian. None of her books had been bestsellers but anyone who appreciated literature knew Marian Foster Todd's work.

"You've got to go to New York!" said Carolina.

"How did she say she knew your parents?" Sally asked.

"Mother. She never talked about Daddy. She says she knew a cousin of Mother's. Or maybe not a cousin. She never really said."

"It's funny that she called you. Such a slim connection."

"She doesn't know anyone else in Albuquerque," Dorothea said. "She claims she was born here."

"Sally, you're the most suspicious person I ever knew," said Carolina.

"And what could she possibly hope to get from Dorothea?" asked Ellen.

In the letters she wrote to Marian in the months following their meeting, Dorothea answered the many questions Marian posed about adoption and growing up with Doug and Bea Browne, and her care for them in their final illnesses. *So loyal and old-fashioned. Loyalty is the quality I admire above all others,* Marian wrote. In her apartment, there was a dear guest room where Dorothea would be quite comfortable. *My front windows overlook the street, and I often stand there to catch a glimpse of our limited northern sky and the comings and goings of my neighbors and the odd assortment of humanity one sees in this quartier. Sometimes I think that if I stood here long enough, I'd see everyone I ever knew and loved—or hated—alive or dead—walk past. Last week the oddest occurrence—I thought I saw a man I once loved very much. He was altered by the years, of course, but something was the same that had always been there. He stopped at one of the excellent houses across the street and stood just long enough for me to study him. By the time I recovered from the shock of seeing him, knowing him after all this time, he was gone. Ours is a story for another time, my dear, for me to tell when you come to visit me.*

One night Marian telephoned and talked about her wardrobe, her books, and her furniture. Really she must get rid of at least half of what she owned; she owned too much of everything.

She'd seen her doctor.

"I went for a perfectly innocent reason, to renew my prescription for sleeping tablets," she said. "He determined that the old trouble's back. They tried before and gave me these past few years. There's nothing left to be done. I was able to see you, thank God."

It took Dorothea a moment to understand that Marian's cancer from ten years before had recurred. She was dying.

"I'll do what anyone would in my position. Put my affairs in order. Hope that when I can no longer care for myself, there will be . . . Dear, would you be kind and send me . . . something from your garden, dried lavender, that kind of thing. Put it in a stocking. If you have no stocking, wrap it in a soft clean cloth."

Dorothea remembered Marian saying, "For God's sake, take better care of yourself."

When Mother was dying, she liked best to have Dorothea with her. Daddy had been that way too. Dorothea didn't have to say or do a thing, just be there. There was nowhere else to go and nothing more important for her to do than just be there.

Sometimes in life you had to take a chance.

"You could come to Albuquerque," Dorothea said. "There's room and—"

She waited for Marian to laugh; a woman of her fame and accomplishment had better places to go at the end of her life than Albuquerque, New Mexico, better than Dorothea's little house behind the blue wall.

"Oh, my dear. I have such a horror of dying without someone

to hold my hand. You are good. You are too good to me, Dorothea.
I don't deserve it."

In preparation for Marian, Dorothea emptied her closet and drawers and moved to the second bedroom.

For all the complications of her life that Marian had confided to Dorothea in their first days together—the many lovers and near-husbands, the stillborn infant, houses bought and sold, possessions scattered and stored on several continents, and papers, so many pieces of paper—Marian traveled lightly to Albuquerque, bringing one ancient red leather suitcase and a white train case.

Her tweed suit had grown too large for her, and when Dorothea helped her undress, the awkwardness Dorothea felt was supplanted by Marian's jaunty exhaustion. Her shriveled breasts hung empty, her belly bulged from her hardened bowels. The muscles in her limbs had withered and the lined skin was slack. Dressed in a gown and robe, Marian seemed too small to be herself. Later that evening, after a few hours of sleep, she insisted on coming to the table to eat. The dogs followed her across the lawn, their tails wagging. She said she knew they would remember her.

Marian liked having Dorothea by her to fetch mugs of tea that cooled untouched on the bedside table. A baby monitor allowed Dorothea to sleep in the other building.

Marian didn't want Dorothea to help her to the bathroom or to bathe her when the time came for that.

"I wasn't there for you when you needed such care," she said one night after an appointment with the doctor recommended by her New York physician. "Now we have to be really practical about this. We must find a woman who is experienced and skilled, one whose services I can afford. A nurse's aide. To spare you, darling. I mustn't disrupt your life."

Sally volunteered at a hospice not far from Dorothea's house, and her suggestion when Dorothea called for advice was that Marian would be taken care of very well if she checked into the hospice; Dorothea could be with her after work every day.

"You're very generous, Dorothea, but you don't know what you're getting into."

Sensible advice, but the whole point of coming to Albuquerque, Marian explained, was to be with Dorothea, to spend precious time with her, however long they had. Besides, in hospice you had to promise to die within a certain time, and it wasn't honorable to make a promise you couldn't keep.

Marian still ate her supper in the dining room. The little walk from one building to the other took forever, and after she crossed the lawn she smiled in triumph. "I've done it again," she said each time. She ate almost nothing. She urged Dorothea to invite friends for dinner, Dolly and Tina, the knitting group, on one occasion the professor from the university who had greeted her at the auditorium door the night of her reading. On that occasion Marian wore a dress instead of her usual kimono. When he left, she confided to those who remained that she was flattered by the man's interest in her work. Sally said, "Marian, you just like men."

The Visiting Angels Agency was recommended by a knitter, and Anna, a small solemn woman with long dark hair, came to Pueblo Luna. She arrived every morning just before Dorothea left for work; often all they did was wave in passing. When she got home, Dorothea heard their voices, mostly English, a little Spanish. On good days, Marian and Anna went looking for shops and restaurants from the past and came home with fudge from the Candy Lady. Marian and Anna festooned the bedroom with long silk scarves and anointed it with perfume. Marian's jewelry hung from every knob and was piled like pirate's treasure on every surface, the bedside table the only sign of the medicinal. No matter how much Anna unpacked from the red leather suitcase, there was more in it and more to display.

They were easy together, but Anna's face went blank when Dorothea entered Marian's bedroom.

"Tell me again," Tina said during coffee break one morning,

"why is it that Marian Foster Todd gets to come to our city and take over your house?"

"She asked me," Dorothea said. "She chose me."

"I know that. But why you? She's a famous old lady, doesn't she have anyone?"

"She's a character, bless her heart," Dolly said. "I can see it from her way but why *you?*"

When Dorothea repeated their questions on knitting night, Sally said, "Maybe she doesn't have anyone else. Or anyone else she likes. I'm not sure that's important right now. She asked. You consented. Now she's here."

Marian's pain deepened and she had less energy. It might have been a stage or the beginning of the end; it was part of the same thing.

"We had such fun," she said one night after Anna left. "Once there was a house near Santa Fe. When you were there, you knew you were really someplace."

"When was this?"

"It was never mine. My ideal of a house ever since. A Mexican house, a line with two wings. Oh, it was lovely. It was the house itself, not the furnishings or anything in it but the house itself, the courtyard. The hills, the valley. We ate every meal outside and we had so much fun."

She closed her eyes. Often in the evening she was overcome, only to wake up before midnight, talkative.

"My parents," Dorothea said. "They were in a house in Santa Fe. Where they found me. Marian, listen. What year was this? What year were you there?"

Marian slept, breathing so softly that Dorothea could hardly hear. It was like this with Marian: Her response was a mountain that lay in the distance no matter how long you walked toward it.

*   *   *

In the other bedroom, Dorothea woke twice each night, after midnight and before the morning alarm.

She slept on a Mexican bed from her father's side of the family and under the Lone Star quilt her maternal grandmother had made. Mother's favorite rocker was in the corner. The wooden arms were splitting where Daddy's refinishing was worn, and when the light hit in just the right way, the stamped name of the chair's manufacturer was visible. Framed snapshots on the walls showed Dorothea in a field of bluebonnets spring after spring on visits to Texas, Dorothea in her senior year in high school, the three of them together.

All her life, Dorothea had been asked about her parents, her real ones, as people said. How real? Not here. They had their reasons.

Even if she'd made a terrible mistake by taking Marian in, when it was over, she could return to her own life. This wouldn't last forever.

Who else had there been to take care of Marian? She needed diapers. She could no longer sit up much less get out of bed and walk unaided.

Marian talked and talked, never about the house in Santa Fe.

News of Marian's illness spread. Writers and poets, academics, movie stars of yesteryear, musicians, old friends, all passing between the coasts, came to say good-bye. The guests had to be welcomed in Marian's well-known style of hospitality; Anna carried out Marian's precise orders. Dorothea did her best to make the guests comfortable and ensure they didn't linger too long at Marian's bedside. The story circulated in New York that Marian was in a private nursing home run by a nun with a star tattooed on her cheek.

Aside from work, Dorothea's time was filled by the nurse's visits, trips to the pharmacy and to stores all over the city for Marian's needs. For someone who was dying, Marian took a great interest in her nails. Anna's niece came to give a weekly manicure and pedicure; Marian's toenails glowed a robust red, her favorite.

For the second time since Marian had come to Pueblo Luna, the knitting group was holding its monthly meeting, this time at Ellen's. That morning, Anna announced that she'd be unable to stay with Marian while Dorothea was at the meeting. She'd promised to do so, yes, but her son who was in the army was coming home and she intended to be there to greet him. At such short notice, it was impossible to round up another Visiting Angel acceptable to Marian.

During lunch in the break room, Dolly and Tina were indignant that Dorothea would miss the meeting, though they dismissed the handicrafters as a bunch of old hippies.

"What else do you have to look forward to, *mujer*? One night away!"

"It's cruel," Dolly said. "Sick people can be cruel. My mother-in-law, bless her heart, everyone walking around in circles for a year before she finally passed. But what can you do?"

"I'll sit with her," Tina announced. "Nothing special tonight."

"Are you sure?" Dorothea asked. "That's so nice of you."

"So now I'm nice? I'm always nice. Haven't you come to my aid? To babysit? To drive the children when I couldn't?"

"I'll come too," Dolly said.

"We'll do it together," Tina said.

"If it's okay with Marian," Dorothea said.

"Of course! It must be agreeable to Marian."

Ellen welcomed the group into her living room, which was crowded with sofas, armchairs, and ottomans similar and dissimilar, like cousins. When things grew quiet, talk turned to Marian.

"She's turned your life upside down," Carolina said.

"There was a house near Santa Fe where they found me. Someone left me there," Dorothea said. "Marian's talked about a house that sounds like the same one but you know Santa Fe, there's so

many houses—" She had decided after long thought that she would
bring up the subject at the meeting.

"Same time?" Ellen asked.

"She won't say."

"You're thinking . . . Wow," Carolina said. "She's your mother?"

"Well," Sally said. "That would explain a lot."

"I've wondered— It did occur to me, who she might be—"

"She could have written a letter," Ellen said. "She could have
done more appropriate things. Coming here, moving in with Dorothea—what an infuriating woman."

"Think about it from her point of view," Sally said. "It might
not be all that easy for her to admit, after all this time, if she is
Dorothea's mother—"

"*Birth* mother," corrected Ellen, who had adopted her daughters. "Why? At this point?"

Sally said, "*Why* doesn't enter the case."

"How brave she'd have to be," said one of the quietest of the
knitters, "to put herself in Dorothea's hands."

Someone sighed, and it occurred to Dorothea that there might
be a woman there who had also left her newborn baby.

When Dorothea returned home, Dolly and Tina reported that
Marian had had a quiet night. She hadn't eaten. She had sipped
gin-and-lime and asked them questions about themselves. "She's
something," Tina said. "A little bit of, you know, a *bruja.*"

Dorothea liked the tangible. She liked the solid wall around her
house and yard. She liked plants taking root and flowering. She did
not like to think of herself as waiting like an overgrown Moses in
the bulrushes for her birth mother to find her. In the dark of the
second bedroom, in the bed from Daddy's side of the family, Dorothea burned with shame.

* * *

Marian took a turn for the worse. The pain shifted from her abdomen to her spine. She was uncomfortable in bed; sitting in a chair was worse. Anna spent hours rubbing lotion on her back. Marian decided to go to the doctor's office; the dogs guarded Marian as she struggled to the car, supported on one side by Dorothea and the other by Anna. She asked Dorothea to stay with her in the examining room and dozed on the paper-covered table while they waited. On the walls, etchings of sailing ships, a chart of diseases of the internal organs, the doctor's degrees. When the doctor appeared, she said that there was nothing left to do but treat the pain. At this stage Marian's pain called for stronger drugs. The hospice nurse would come to the house later that day.

"How long?" Marian asked.

"There's the pressure on your lungs. The strain on your heart. I can't tell you exactly."

"Tell me."

"Less than a month," the doctor said. "More than a week."

"You're not a very accomplished liar," Marian said. "It will be much sooner. Very wise. Never take away a person's hope. No one has that right."

Different drugs came, for pain, for anxiety, for this and that, but nothing to stop death. Dorothea brought a tape recorder to Marian's room, and at night Marian's favorite Bach concerto played until Marian cried, "Stop! Stop!" In her drugged state, Marian called out commands—*rue, camino, viale*—as if she were giving directions to a taxi driver. There were fewer occasions when Marian recognized Dorothea or said her name. Dorothea asked, "Which house in Santa Fe? Who was with you?"

One morning when it was especially clear and the sky a heartbreaking blue, Dorothea stopped at the bedroom door to tell Anna she was going to work.

"It's now," Anna said.

Dorothea held one hand, Anna the other, while Marian died.

*　　*　　*

At first, the dogs looked for Marian. After a few days they didn't. The little house with the bedroom and garden had been theirs before; it was theirs again. Circling one corner of the bedroom, circling the other, they found their places and slept.

Marian had dictated her will to an Albuquerque lawyer. Everything was Dorothea's now. *To Dorothea Browne: She acted so much like a daughter that she is mine.* Anna had witnessed the will. She told Dorothea that Marian had even dictated the punctuation. There was nothing for Anna in the will.

After Marian's cremation, Dorothea selected a string of big pearls from the white train case Marian had carried to Albuquerque. She'd been through Marian's things more than once and had found nothing of interest. Dorothea invited Anna to come by the house.

When Anna arrived she announced that she didn't have time to stay. She was working for an old man in Corrales, and he wasn't doing so well. His family was mostly in northern New Mexico. The old man had moved to Albuquerque years before to teach high school history. There had been talk of taking him back home. Now it was too late.

"I have something for you," Dorothea said.

Holding out the pearls, Dorothea knew that she had made a mistake not wrapping them as a gift. The companionship Anna had given Marian in her last weeks had no price. The pearls were inadequate, and possibly not real.

"Thank you," Anna said. She was a courteous woman. "I have to leave now. The ride to Corrales."

"Anna— Did Marian talk about me? Did she say anything about . . ."

Anna thought before she answered.

"She appreciated you and everything you did for her. She said many times that she wished she had a daughter like you. But she also said often that she wished you dressed better. And took better care of your skin."

*　　*　　*

A few weeks later, a letter came from Marian's New York lawyer to inform Dorothea that there were matters Marian had left dangling. Though most of her papers had already gone to libraries and archives, there was the remainder to be distributed to a place of Dorothea's choice, as well as personal photographs. A decision had to be made about the floor-through in the Village. As Marian's heir, Dorothea could occupy it for the remainder of the long lease; however Dorothea wished to dispose of the apartment, the estate was responsible for paying the monthly rent. The apartment was full of Marian's extensive wardrobe and her jewelry; the furniture, rugs, china, and glassware; the books collected over the length of her long life. It was necessary for Dorothea to sort through Marian's things in New York.

Sally and the others said, and Tina and Dolly agreed, that once she was in New York, Dorothea should just keep going. Cross the ocean to Europe. To the rest of the world. Live her own life at last. Even that miracle might be waiting for Dorothea.

Once there, Dorothea would make up her mind. It was her turn now to stand at the front window of Marian's apartment and look across at the brick buildings, at the bright flowers in the window boxes. Once there, Dorothea would take her time. The life that she was living, and the person that she had always been, demanded that consideration.

THIRD TRIO

The Blue Birds Come Today

Plum Creek

The Mother Who Stayed

The Blue Birds Come Today

O n a bright clear morning in November 1874, Hiram Rathbun traveled across the Hudson to the blacksmith in Schuylerville. Most of the work on his farm Hiram did himself, but the anvil called for the skill of the smith, and so he set off down the mountain.

While he was at the blacksmith's, Hiram chose a pattern for a wrought-iron fence for the family graveyard on the Intervale, the road that ran past his brother Lyman's farm. The twisted uprights were divided by three lozenges, the first bulging out at the sides, the middle a simple oval, the topmost echoing the angle of the first and ending in a fleur-de-lis. The graves were on a rise above the Intervale so Hiram passed them every time he went to his brother's farm.

The oldest graves were those of Hiram's grandparents, Paul and Patience, who were born in the last century when the country was still a colony. The newer graves were those of Hiram's children.

Baby Lyman's gravestone bore his name and one date, *1862.* Albert E. was dead at age four and Eunicy before she reached that age. Annie Sophia's time was recorded carefully: *16 years, 7 months, 3 days.* The second Albert and his brother Almont were together in a grave; they were part of a set of triplets.

In spring and summer, Hiram's wife, Mary Ann, and their youngest children set flowers in the graveyard. Alfred, the third of the triplets, was ten this year. The second Annie was fifteen, and the second Eunicy, the youngest and the last of Hiram's children, was nine.

The fence would be ready in the spring.

By the time the restored anvil was in the wagon and Hiram reversing his morning journey, the sky was as gray as the winter awaiting him, and cold rain fell in sheets. It was all he could do to get across the river. The water below him and the water from above seemed so much the same that he feared Doll would misstep and tip them both—and wagon and anvil—into the river. Safe on the other side, he knew that whether or not he and Doll found shelter, they wouldn't be home that night.

Warren Sherman was closest. When Hiram arrived, Warren was in the barnyard, finishing up chores. He was someone Hiram had known all his life, a bachelor Hiram spoke to twice a year at most. They were the same age, fifty-one, but their lives had taken different paths; Hiram was the father of sixteen children, ten living. With his older sons, Hiram farmed five hundred acres to Warren's one hundred.

Warren welcomed Hiram and shared with him the thick stew made from a chicken he'd killed that morning. They ate in Warren's kitchen, where bunches of herbs and other plants were hung to dry. Warren, like Hiram's wife, Mary Ann, had a way with arrangement, keeping his dishes and cups in good order on the shelves, smallest to largest, left to right. After the dish of stew, they talked by candlelight, the smoke from Warren's pipe rising and disappearing into the darkness. Warren provided Hiram with the hired man's bed; the poor fellow was visiting his ailing mother in Vermont.

The next morning was clear, and Hiram set off for home.

In 1840, thirty-four years before, Hiram Rathbun had married Mary Ann Rumbold when both were seventeen.

He had been born on his father's farm in Easton, county of Washington, state of New York. Coming from Lancashire, settling first in Rhode Island, the Rathbuns had been in Easton before stone fences defined boundaries for the animals and people.

Mary Ann came to America from London at the age of seven. She spoke with only a hint of an accent, on the word *bath* in particular.

They met while Mary Ann was visiting distant relatives in Troy, city people who rode over to Easton in the fall to enjoy the expanse of color on the hills and open country, and to walk up the slope of the mountain where the Rathbun family had farmed for two generations.

For as long as they were able, Hiram and Mary Ann Rathbun took the long walk around the mountain in the fall to celebrate their chance meeting.

After she married Hiram, Mary Ann formed the habit of keeping a diary to record the weather, births and deaths, neighborly visits, the work done. She wrote in pencil on the seven lines provided for each day in the black Standard diary. Someone—Hiram at first, later a child or grandchild—made her a gift of one each year.

Like many country people, Mary Ann Rathbun tracked the movement of the seasons by the birds. In March 1874 she wrote in her diary that *the blue birds come today,* and in May she made note of the appearance of bobolinks and swallows. Another year, when there was an especially warm Saturday in March: *Robins Blue Birds Butterflies and everything else.*

One year Mary Ann kept a bird in a cage and wrote *birdseed* in her accounts on the last pages of the diary.

Today the Bird got out of his Cage today he come back again.

All the Rathbun children were at the breakfast table on Election Day 1874 except for the firstborn. In the spring, Piney had moved west with her husband, Henry Witbeck, and their son, Little Charlie.

The youngest Rathbuns were Alfred, Eunicy, and Annie. The older children—Kenyon, Stevie, Lewis, Lois, Jennie, and Alta—ranged in age from twenty-seven to eighteen.

It snowed that morning in 1874.

After the chores were done, Mary Ann got Kenyon and Stevie to carry the plants inside the house.

By eight o'clock, the men were setting out for Election, and Eunicy and Annie scattered to play.

While the men and boys were away from home, the girls cleaned their room and the boys' room, airing them for the last time until spring.

Mary Ann's bedroom was the north front room overlooking the valley. The plaster walls were unfinished. There was always something more pressing to do, though she'd bought wallpaper in the summer with her bedroom in mind. Mary Ann remembered the task on her nightly return to her bedroom, when it was too late and she had done what she could.

Election morning, daylight hours lay ahead. She brought out the rolls of paper and lined them up against the wall. Mary Ann called to the girls to come help her.

There was discussion between Jennie and Lois about whether or not it would be better to put all the furniture in the center of the room or in the stairwell. Mary Ann listened until the heat was gone from their talk, then told them to carry the bedding down to the sitting room. She and Father would sleep there that night. The rest of the furniture would rest in the stairwell but they'd keep the long table. And when they were done with that, would they please carry up the wooden ladder? She told Alta to stay with her to help prepare the room for the cutting, pasting, and setting of the wallpaper.

They all agreed that the pattern of the paper was fanciful. The roses were pale pink and in bloom with red curves to indicate the petals. The stems of the roses were right but the leaves were those of parsley, not right. Against the yellow ground was a deeper yellow flower, an unopened bud very like the chamomile that grew on the west side of the house.

The paste was made in batches—flour, water, alum, and oil of cloves—and carried upstairs. All the girls and Mary Ann took turns on the ladder. The paper had to be positioned just right but mustn't be pressed to the wall too soon or the paste would form lumps. Alta was the most careful and had the most delicate touch, but she couldn't stand long with her arms stretched above her. The position started her coughing, or it was the smell of the paste that afflicted her. Alta descended until she recovered, then claimed her turn again. Lois declared that Alta was also best at laying the paste evenly when the paper was rolled out and measured in sections. Eunicy and Annie were put in charge of keeping the scraps clean and dry in case patching was required.

Arms and necks aching, they admired their finished work just before darkness came. In the winter, they would sew window curtains and a valance for the bed from the machine lace Mary Ann had bought that summer.

The next morning, Kenyon and Stevie found Old Tommy dead in the barn, and the men talked at breakfast about how soon Doll would join her mate.

* * *

Dahlias, asters, bachelor's buttons, Jacob's ladders were still in bloom. *One night soon, Jack Frost will nip them,* Mary Ann wrote in her diary later in the week, the day she preserved the last of the quinces.

All year round they prepared for winter: in the summer cutting wood and leaving it to dry; in summer and early fall picking and preserving strawberries, huckleberries, black and red raspberries, apples and peaches, and plums, also cherries to be dried and canned, grapes for wine and raisins, red currants for preserves and wine; cutting sage and drying it; chestnutting in October, putting up corn, tomatoes stewed, pickled, and spiced, string beans, greens, beets, turnips, cabbage, and butter beans. They piled hay around the carrots and sprouts, which they left in the garden until the snows covered the ground. Those root vegetables tasted better after a frost. They ran candles dozens at a time.

The farm and their own labors provided them with honey, butter, eggs, milk, and cheese. There were chickens, pigs, turkeys, also cattle and sheep for veal and lamb, beef and mutton. The boys fished in the Hudson and Battenkill rivers and brought home trout and other fresh fish for dinner. In fall, they boiled cider from the apple trees near the barn. Mary Ann and her daughters, and later the hired girls, baked bread, pies, cookies, and cakes: Coconut cake, fried cookies, fruit cake, marble cake, ginger cake, jelly cake, raisin cake, shortcake, white cake, sugar cake. When they killed the pigs, they cut up the pork, made sausage, and tried out the lard.

Their crops were sold in Schuylerville and Schaghticoke from the back of the wagon: buckwheat, corn, flax, oats, potatoes, wheat. The wool they sheared from their sheep was sold to the Joslins in Buskirk. They cut hay for their animals' winter. The geese were sold for the holiday table and their feathers used in comforters and pillows.

Some things had to be bought. Cloth for the jackets, trousers, dresses, chemises, petticoats, nightgowns, underwear for the men and the women; yarn for the socks knitted at home; wallpaper, also machine-made lace for the curtains in the sitting room and Mary Ann and Hiram's bedroom. Molasses, coffee, salt, and sugar, coconut, chocolate, and ginger, came from far away and required cash. Once in a great while Hiram bought oysters and clams, which were hauled on ice by wagon over the mountains from the Massachusetts shore.

In 1874 alone, Mary Ann and her daughters sewed aprons and sunbonnets, bed ticks, blouses and capes, chemises and other undergarments, comforters, drawers, waists and vests, wrappers and dresses. The dresses were brown, black, silk, calico, and one was black alpaca. They sewed flannel petticoats and shirts, a Jimmy (as they called the canvas work jackets the men wore), nightcaps and nightgowns. They knit stockings of cotton and wool, and socks for the men. One overcoat was made that year, for Lewis, and they sewed pants for all the men. They made towels for the family, and quilts. First the quilt blocks, then the lining, then they pieced it all together. For Jennie they made a basket quilt and for Lois a log cabin. The family's shoes, belts, and boots were made at home.

Mary Ann made carpet rags and hard soap, ironed clothes, made straw and feather ticks. They washed the carpets and laid them out to dry. Mr. Quackenbush came and grained the upstairs trim so it looked like oak. Kenyon installed a sink and a tub. Walls were painted, plastered, and whitewashed.

On November thirtieth the old clock struck at half past nine in the morning. It had been silent for years and unheard from thereafter.

December 1874, Thursday 10
Father and Eunicy washed
part of the Cloths it rained
all day

we all done what we could

And so for years she had written: *I done all I could. I done what I could. I done a little of everything.* She meant: done ironing, knitting, cooking, baking, mending, washing, cleaning, sewing. She wrote: *We all done what we could.* On a good day, she called the weather *pleasant.* She wrote: *The work got done in good season.*

Visitors came to the farm high up on its hill, on Sunday and other days. Visits to the farm far outnumbered the visits Mary Ann returned. Among the visitors were relations and friends, too numerous to say of them any more than their names: Aunt Lois Tripp and Herbert R. Tripp, Aunt Sarah Harrington, Grandma Perlina Rathbun, Mr. and Mrs. J. T. Wilcox, Miss Button, Miss Phebe Freeman of Coila, Mr. Chubb and Mr. Hurd, Mr. Eddy and Mr. Rose, Mr. Van Pelt; also Mr. and Mrs. Presward Brownell from Delaware County in Iowa, Myra Ann and her husband Hat, Will and Ella Tucker, and Will Taylor. One Sunday in December, Mary Ann Rathbun recorded in her diary that it was "a long lonesome day." Three visitors, and it was cloudy and cold.

In the course of 1874, members of the Rathbun family traveled to Battenville; Bennington; Buskirk; West Cambridge, South Cambridge, and Cambridge; Greenwich; Hoosick Falls; Schuylerville; Saratoga Springs; Crandalls Corners; Johnsonville; and Troy.

In the midst of her preparations for moving west with her family, Piney had found the time to cut out a dress for her sister Alta; Lois and Jennie sewed it. Piney's mother and sisters made her a comforter and a quilt, and helped to sew clothing for Little Charlie, just a year old. Piney sewed herself a calico dress before leaving the farm where she was born.

Piney, Henry, and Little Charlie went to Greenwich on May 20, 1874, to have their picture taken before they left. By June 12 Mary

Ann received Piney's first letter from the West and she answered it the next day.

Lewis Rathbun, who was 22, began his life of wandering by traveling in 1874 to Indiana, Connecticut, and Vermont, in later years following his sister Piney and her family as far west as Minnesota. On almost every June 4 Mary Ann would mark his initials, *LR,* in her diary and write that it was his birthday. In 1874, his mother and his sister Alta got letters from him in May, July, and August. He sent a picture of himself. Lewis came home on December 5, left again on January 26, 1875, and would return on February 5. He stayed on until May 12, 1875, when he took off again for the West. In the years to follow, if he did come home it was in December.

In September 1874, Stevie and his sister Lois took the Excursion to the east portal of the Hoosac Tunnel. Once the tunnel was completed, the railroad would speed goods from the West to Troy and Albany and through the Hoosac Mountains to Boston. Seven hundred and fifty men, Irishmen mostly, some Cornishmen, all experienced miners, were building the tunnel. The summer of 1867, sixteen men had died after the explosion of an experimental lighting machine. In 1869, three men died when five hundred pounds of nitroglycerine exploded.

That September had all the richness and bounty of summer overlaid with the poignancy of death. The chilled air of the underground world reached their nostrils from the tunnel's portal. The opening into the earth was twenty feet high and twenty-four feet wide. To be sure, there were barns at home larger than that, but this wasn't made of wood to be sawn and hammered but rock, this was the thick rock of the Earth itself.

*   *   *

On January 27, 1874, when the year was still young, Mary Ann had taken Alta to see Dr. Langworthy in Greenwich, and they got some medicine from Mr. Tefft, paying forty-eight cents for it. Alta went with her father on February 4, got a different medicine, and Hiram paid the doctor two dollars. A week later, she returned with her brother Kenyon to see the doctor and get still more medicine.

On her fourth visit, February 26, the doctor gave Alta three kinds of medicine. While she was in town, she bought cloth, buttons, and thread.

On March 5, Mary Ann went with Alta to see Dr. Langworthy, and they got medicine. March 20, Hiram went for more medicine.

By April 17, no more trips to the doctor, no more medicine. Alta sewed an apron for her little sister Annie and went with her mother to Greenwich to shop for thread and cloth, and to go to the bank. They went together to the Corners to pay the insurance money. Hiram made Alta a new pair of shoes in June. One Sunday she went to the Society of Friends with her brother Kenyon, whose habit it was to visit different churches.

That summer Alta made visits to Miss Button, to Eliza Ann Watters, and she stayed for over a week with her uncle Elisha.

In September, Alta planted seeds for spring flowers. By September, winter was in the air.

In October, the family got a letter from Piney; Little Charlie had died on September 2.

Alta started a new medicine, and soon started another, this one made by Mary Ann. Alta was occupied tying a comforter and being fitted for a new dress by her mother and older sisters. They worked together to make clothes for Jennie. Alta helped at home doing all the work she could, and she looked after the younger children. She ran candles, eight dozen in two days in November, the same day the turkeys were killed. In December, her brother Lewis arrived home from his latest trip in time to help kill the pigs. On the last day of the year, Alta knitted him a pair of socks. On January 3, 1875,

Jennie married Willie Sprague, who owned a farm on the North Greenwich Road and also a meat market in town.

The time after the New Year was always low; the air was cold and damp. Morning came late and night came early. All the younger children came down with chicken pox, nothing to be done for them but stop them from scratching and keep them comfortable. Mid-January was the worst; after that, the red spots began to heal and the itching no longer drove them to distraction. On January 26, Lewis left for Connecticut. Ordinary days came, one much like the other. Alta was worn from her care of the sick, and when they developed whooping cough she did, too. It was the kind that made a noise and wracked the body, so that she and the children were heard around the house.

On February 9, Kenyon was sent to town and Doctor Hults, a new doctor for Alta, came to the farm February 10. Alta died the next day, February 11, 1875. Alta was buried in the family graveyard. When Alta's stone was set on her grave, her name and the span of her life were on it: *Alta S. Died February 11, 1875 18 years 3 months.*

The Rathbuns' neighbor Richard Harrington died the same day as Alta. He was buried five days later, and Mary Ann made note of it in her diary, though she wrote nothing about Alta's death or burial.

Jennie, so recently become Mrs. Sprague, came back to the farm and stayed with Mary Ann for three days. It was cold and bright that week, measuring ten below one day.

Mary Ann had days when she didn't rise from her bed and days when she was as she'd always been.

In the spring, Hiram went back over the river to the blacksmith in Schuylerville and picked up the fencing he'd ordered for the graveyard on the rise just west of Lyman's brick farmhouse. Alta's father and brothers dug postholes and installed the new fence. When neighbors passed, they slowed to admire it.

Before the fence was in place, the graves were invisible behind the tiger lilies, wild roses, and daisies of summer, and hidden by the blazing color of fall. Only in the winter did the stones show to those riding by, and even then they sometimes were no more than the shadows they cast on the mounds of snow. The fence called your attention to the graveyard and gave you something to think about.

Plum Creek

D inah was in charge of herself. She did her homework and fixed dinner every day but Sunday—not too much for a nine-year-old going on ten, not if the nine-year-old was Dinah, her father said. At school she was in third grade, reading books with chapters and no pictures, and mastering multiplication. When the afternoon school bus dropped Dinah at the ranch gate, she walked the quarter mile to the low-water bridge across Plum Creek, where Mama's more-or-less-terrier Bird waited under a live oak, rain or shine. Once Dinah crossed the creek, she was home.

Dinah knew that doing things in a regular way made time pass. The minute she got to the house, she changed her school dress for dungarees, checked that the meat for dinner was truly thawing and that they had their starch, usually rice. Daddy didn't get home until six. His work as a county extension agent took him from one end of the county to the other. His office was all the way in Luling, the next big town.

Because Mama had left them in the spring when the bluebonnets were starting and before the garden amounted to much, the first few months she was gone, Dinah picked their dinner vegetables from the big bags of English peas, green beans, and broccoli in the freezer. Most afternoons, Dinah raced through her homework at the kitchen table with a pair of binoculars by her side to watch for a squirrel they called Nacho because his ear had been cut in a fight. Bird waited with only a small show of impatience—a twitch of her tail, her brown eyes slantwise to check on Dinah. After homework, they'd head out to see what the day had done. They inspected Daddy's flats of seedlings on the big plywood tables on sawhorses. They checked the clematis on the fence, the mountain laurel, and the Mexican plum, the first to bloom each year, and then they took off around the ranch and into the woods, returning in time to cook dinner. In the brief moment after she opened the kitchen door, Dinah couldn't help herself. She looked for her mother.

Dinah had no clear idea of why her mother was gone; she had memories of voices in the night and talk of money, money, money, money. Once, Moira told Dinah, *Your daddy's not the least bit ambitious, so you and I must do our best with second-best.* Another time, there was a door flung open, a sudden shaft of light in her dark bedroom, and the sound of loud voices when her mother and father thought she slept. Try as she might, Dinah couldn't hear their words. Dinah pictured her mother in the vegetable garden and when she held the image long enough she heard Moira sighing, but her mother might as easily have sighed from being hot and tired as from yearning for a different life with a man who was ambitious and gave her first-best. Whatever her mother's reasons, Dinah's imagination couldn't take her past the irreducible fact that one day she came home from school and her mother was gone.

D. R., Dinah's father, claimed that he had little interest in people. The world that held him was botanical. Hybrids and imports inspired his scorn; he respected the uncultivated natives. If he had his way, he once told Dinah, he'd spend his life wandering and be happy if he saw even half of the species to be found across Texas.

D. R. had graduated from Texas A&M University, his father's alma mater, in the mid-1930s. D. R.'s father had died at an early age, electrocuted in a farm accident. It wasn't a question of whether D. R. would attend A&M; it was a given. He majored in plants—as he called the science of growing bigger, better, and more bug-resistant crops to feed the increasing numbers of livestock and people—and after graduation he became a county extension agent and worked in one rural area of Texas after another.

David Rangel Warren, called D. R., met Dinah's mother, Moira O'Brien, when he was in Fort Worth for a convention. He married her and took her west where there were plant-devouring cattle and money-producing oil fields, and then to counties south where there was so much land, all of it flat, that it was like standing on a great ocean. There, crops tore up the native habitat and cattle overgrazed. Moira's family had not wanted her to marry D. R. They had toiled for decades in Fort Worth, selling automobiles for a harvest of cash, and wanted her to have a businessman or a banker for a husband.

In driving from ranch to ranch, small town to small town, Dinah's father became a keen observer of the landscape. Anyone who wasn't blind could see the bluebonnets and Indian paintbrushes blanketing in spring, but D. R.'s view was keener; he taught Dinah to read the signs the plants gave in their cycle.

D. R.'s longest assignment, the one he said he would retire from, was in Central Texas, Caldwell County, thirty miles south of Austin. In exchange for minimal caretaking duties, he and Moira and Dinah lived on a ranch on Plum Creek. There he conceived the idea of saving at least one Texas wildflower from what he called the three horsemen: cattle, highways, and development. He chose *Amoreuxia wrightii*, the fragile Yellowshow, and began by gathering seeds and finding the best conditions to propagate them in pots, flats, and beds. He collected the Yellowshow's tiny seeds and distributed them free of charge to whoever would take them. Because of his conviction that the abundant wildflowers of Texas were in grave danger, D. R. endured the amusement of his fellow citizens, and Dinah went through school as the daughter of a crank.

One afternoon, when the school bus pulled up to the ranch gate, Bird wasn't waiting for Dinah under the live oak. Mr. Christie, the bus driver, took a look at the sky and ordered Dinah to get to the house and stay there.

"Go to the center of the house," he told her. "Don't tarry. Tornado possibilities."

Daddy always said that Vernon Christie looked for the cloud and ignored the silver lining, but that afternoon the sky was as green as a lima bean, and it throbbed as if something wanted out.

When Dinah got to the house, Bird was there. The dog wormed inside the kitchen before Dinah opened the door more than a crack. Bird hated thunder, lightning, and rain, and probably wasn't fond of tornadoes. She didn't fear snakes, though, and alerted Dinah to rattlers on their walks. Now she was whining. Maybe she could hear the tornado and Dinah couldn't. Dinah noticed at that moment how very still everything was and then she heard a new noise like a train far off but coming closer, the biggest train the world had ever known, bearing down on them.

Go to the center of the house, but where was that?

They had no storm cellar. They had no cellar at all. The house rested on cedar posts.

Not upstairs, which was all Dinah's, all three rooms now that Mama was gone and Daddy had moved downstairs.

Not the porch or the kitchen or Daddy's room.

Bird was whimpering. The house had two windows on each of its four sides. The windows matched, up and down, so many windows, windows all around. Dinah checked the kitchen clock, as if the tornado were a real train, due any minute, and she and Bird might miss it. The fur along the ridge of Bird's spine was standing straight up. Dinah ran into the hall and opened the door of the big closet. Bird pushed past, and Dinah closed the door behind them. The sound of the train was muffled in the dark among the suitcases and cardboard boxes. Dinah found a free place at the back of the closet and sat with her knees to her chin, her head touching the hems of jackets and coats hanging empty above them. Bird leaned into Dinah, shivering like she was cold through and through, and smelling like earth. There was another smell in the closet, a familiar one, sweet and brisk and maybe something sharp beneath the sweetness: Mama in the garden brushing a drop of sweat away and inspecting the row she'd hoed with a look on her face that said her own storm of temper and discontent was coming.

One day, Dinah had arrived home from school and her mother's things were gone. Clothes gone. Bible gone. And gone was the embroidered runner Mama kept on her vanity, along with the jars of Noxema and Jergens Lotion and her bottle of lily of the valley cologne, her silver-backed brush, and the Breck shampoo bottle from the side of the bathtub. Where were all of Mama's things, Dinah had wondered. And where was Mama herself? Dinah's father didn't make it possible to voice either question.

Now, in the wind and the howling of the train, in the pounding of the metal roof trying to free itself, Dinah's first question was answered by the boxes that her father in his fury and misery had shut in the closet. Now, when the sounds were bearing down upon her, Dinah was grateful for her mother's presence even if it was just her things. If she closed her eyes and breathed in as deep as she could, Dinah might catch the train.

The tornado came close, knocking down their mailbox, taking the scrubby trees alongside the road, missing the house, missing Dinah and the dog.

Two years later, Moira's oldest brother telephoned one Thursday night while D. R. and Dinah were listening to *The Lone Ranger,* to say that Moira was dead. Inexplicably, she had been living in Los Angeles, and her car had been hit by a truck on her way to work. Her body was with her parents, and if D. R. wanted to attend the funeral he'd better get to Fort Worth in a hurry.

The church in Fort Worth had tall white columns in front.

D. R. wouldn't let go of Dinah's hand as he walked her down the aisle and sat her close to the altar. They were just one row behind the family, and the sight of Moira's well-known features on their unsmiling faces—her long nose and the shape of her eyes—was dizzying. As soon as Dinah got settled, her grandmother turned around and called her by name, telling Dinah to go up front to pay her respects to her mother. The top of the casket was closed. Dinah took courage and touched her hand to the polished wooden surface. The coffin looked both too small and too large. Dinah couldn't decide whether or not it was a good fit for Moira, but then, she wasn't convinced that her mother was inside.

The sermon and the prayers were nothing that couldn't have been said of any human being who'd been born and died.

Dinah and D. R. rode out to the cemetery in the pickup, following the hearse and the limousines, and after the cemetery, at Dinah's grandmother's invitation, they went to the house, which was grander than the best houses in their town, even though it was the county seat. When the guests left, and the food and drink had been cleared away by a maid in a white apron, the family sat in the living room. Dinah had eaten too many lemon bars, but she knew better than to complain to her father.

"We can offer Dinah things you can't, David," her grandmother was saying. "And we'd like nothing more than to have her with us. We've had this discussion before—"

"I haven't forgotten your kind offers," D. R. said in the accepting tone he used for the weather and the failure of an experiment. Dinah wondered when these offers had been made. D. R. was next to Dinah on a plush couch, dressed in his one suit, a white shirt, and the red tie he'd ironed that morning. A strand of enormous pearls curled on her grandmother's bosom. City and country, her grandmother and father might as well have been from separate galaxies.

"We can educate the girl," an uncle said. He was the one closest to Moira in age, the one who looked most like her, and Dinah concentrated on his eyebrows. "Fort Worth has a lot to offer a girl like Dinah. Dancing lessons. Piano. Or another instrument if she prefers. We have the resources. We can send her to college in the East. She'll have real opportunity."

Dinah was in no way musical. Dancing was not her strong suit. She knew they wouldn't let her keep her mother's dog, and in that moment the after-school walks with Bird seemed precious above all else. Besides, who would see that dinner was waiting for her father?

Her grandfather's voice was gravelly, like he hadn't talked in days. "If Dinah doesn't come live with us, that's the end of it. No money from this family, no trust fund, no inheritance. Not a dime."

Dinah's father got up from his chair. "Your offer is generous," he said. "I appreciate it. Still and all, I don't think making a rich orphan of Dinah is any solution."

Only then did D. R. look at Dinah, but she was already on her feet. She gave a curtsey, the best she could manage, and raised her hand in a wave. She couldn't do what manners dictated and kiss her grandparents and uncles farewell. She walked out beside her father and drove with him home to Plum Creek.

The Mother Who Stayed

Dinah changes her mind, first the fuzzy sweater, then the silk shirt, and she ends up in her uniform of charcoal turtleneck, black pants, and the earrings made from gold buttons. She runs her hand through her silver hair, brushes a line along the edge of each eyelid, and pencils in her lips. She dabs perfume on her wrists and, scented with violets, is dressed at last. Still, she hesitates.

She feels late for dinner at Grace's, so she takes the shortcut at King Road, turning at the brick house that was for sale when they were looking last year. Taylor ruled against it, choosing their farmhouse at the end of its own rough lane off a back road. She passes the horse farm with the white wooden fences, and the next farm where the road curves so sharply that barn and house sit face-to-face. The winter night is dark, the houses few and far between. Five miles through the woods, a yellow road sign at a dead end shines in the headlights, its black arrow going two ways. Grace's house is miles away, somewhere over the hills, over the covered bridge, the other side of the icy river.

The headlights barely dent the darkness beyond the arrow. There's a light far off; Dinah turns toward it but when she reaches the long driveway she knows that she won't ask directions. She backtracks to the double arrow and sees River Road, which has been there all along.

It's pitch-black by the river, but she recognizes the two houses she passes, blank yellow and blank white in her headlights. Some years, the river floods over their doorsteps.

A mile more and there's the covered bridge. Each plank thumps as the car passes over, like heartbeats underwater.

Seeing the familiar from a different angle. Not recognizing one friend because you expect to see another. She wakes every morning, wondering what's wrong and remembering that Taylor's dead.

Taylor's favorite room in their house was the library, and there he died, in his chair by the fire. His pile of books was by his side, his laden shelves around him and the windows bare to the corral between the silver barns, the old stone wall peeking above mounds of snow, the hill reaching the cloudy sky.

Dinah was upstairs with a paint color chart, looking through yellows, the yellows of butter and egg yolks, of lemon skin, and the pale meat of Florida grapefruit, the rosy yellow of a perfect ripe peach. The farmhouse was so very plain that she could bring the color up to the ceiling, over the doorjambs and windowsills— flat for the ceiling, eggshell for the walls, enamel for the trim. She knew how the colors would look, even in unfamiliar northern light. Painting the upstairs was the last thing to be done. Taylor said that when she settled on the colors, she'd settle down for good.

From the smallest room, Dinah retrieved a box; one of the workers had found it the previous summer. She carried it downstairs and set it on the kitchen table. She considered making coffee but thought she'd had enough. Inside the box were notebooks no bigger than her hand, some with leather covers as soft as talcum powder. The books reeked of age.

"August 10 1877 this morning I carried aunt Phebe over to Alvins

she had gone to the see Shore. The seashore. What do you think of that?" Dinah called to Taylor. When he didn't answer, she looked into the next room, where he sat with his back to her, hidden in his favorite wing chair.

It was quiet in the house, not even the hum of the refrigerator.

A burning log split and toppled. A spark escaped through the fire screen to the hearthstone.

She went into the library, knelt and patted out the spark, rubbed ash into the marble.

Only then did Dinah look up. Taylor's chin was on his chest. He was crushing his book. Dinah pushed him back against the chair and tilted his head to open his air passage. She took the book from his lap and laid it facedown on the floor, keeping his place.

"It's okay," she told Taylor.

She touched his face and felt his neck for a pulse. She touched his wrist. She lowered her head to his silent heart.

The sounds of the house resumed, and the calls of the crows as they flew over the open fields.

Adler opened the front door, hugged her to him, and maneuvered her inside the house. He wore his battered tweed golf cap, as he did all winter to protect his bald head.

The wall by the coat closet was covered with photographs from Grace's life: the house when she first bought it on her graduation from college, favorite students from the school where she'd taught French and where Adler had once been headmaster. Dinah, freshman year, face raised to her first real snowfall. Grace's first vegetable garden. Dinah and Taylor in bright sunshine, she wearing a lacy dress, he in a white linen suit, only a little taller than she, his fine hair fallen over his eyes.

Grace stood at the stove, her hair gathered in a complicated bun low on her neck. Steam rose from a pot of boiling water.

In Grace's house the walls were an old white, and the furniture was dark and wooden, with chenille, velvet, and homespun linen in gray and violet for the upholstery and drapes. The rugs tried to follow Grace's orders, though they hinted of rose. Grace had made these decisions a long time ago and saw no reason to change a thing.

Adler handed Dinah a glass of red wine. "I found this in Saratoga," he said, "tell me what you think," and settled her into a chair at the long kitchen table. He started to fill her in on weather predictions and car accidents, news culled from his morning coffee at the town bakery.

Two sets of headlights pulled up at the house.

The other dinner guests unwound from their scarves, boots, and coats, and came into the big kitchen, cheeks and noses red from the cold.

The younger man—"Keith Wright," Grace said—glanced at Dinah and walked past her to inspect a small painting of a turkey. He was built like a bulldog, with muscular biceps, massive shoulders tapering to skinny legs, his tight gray sweater emphasizing his broad chest. His dark hair was thinning and slicked back. He was a handsome young man who was trying to look tough. Dinah pulled her eyes from him.

Next came Amber Mattingley, small and trim to the bone, brown eyes and pale skin, and auburn hair. She gave a polite smile when she was introduced to Dinah and looked around, looking for something, then set the book she was carrying on a pile of magazines.

John Malcolm Connor, stark white hair and ice-blue eyes, towered over Dinah and shook her hand.

It was Grace's way when she had people to dinner in winter to lead her company through the dining room, past the round table— set and inviting—into the living room for wine before the fire, but now Grace announced, "I'm off schedule. I put the pasta in too soon. Sit down so I can serve it before it gets cold. Have your wine at the table," and Adler said, "*Al tavolo! Al tavolo!*"

In the dining room, the drapes were drawn against the night.

"I'm here," Grace said. "John, next to me. I haven't seen you for weeks."

With little fuss, Grace seated the guests and Adler put bowls of pasta with a venison and tomato sauce before them, and the meal began.

Amber and Dinah were side by side. Dinah spread her napkin on her lap, tasted the wine, and asked Amber if she was from the area.

Amber said, "My family used to be. My mother said. A great-great-grandfather. Or a great-great-great. He abandoned my great-great-grandmother in Ohio. He ran away to be a private detective." Her voice was light and childish. "Keith brought me here," Amber said. Across the table, he was listening to Grace while John Malcolm listened to Adler. Dinah recalled Grace saying that John Malcolm's wife was dead. She'd been a writer; one of her books was in the pile by Taylor's chair.

"Keith's friend Sam inherited this big estate. The house got destroyed sometime and most of the land was sold off. The marble's still there from the house. It started snowing the minute we got here in November! Part of the second story's still there, and there's the big beams, all down on the ground. How they got the marble up that hill, I don't know. Horses, Keith says."

The land bordered on national forest. There was nothing but trees beyond them, few neighbors on the road before them.

The girl was brave, Dinah thought. Or else she'd been kidnapped. She looked like the kind of girl who'd let herself be kidnapped.

"Keith's fixing up the cottage we're in, in exchange for rent. Sam pays for materials and it's labor that gets you, Keith says. Keith's really a photographer so this is a better deal for him."

Amber checked across the table; Keith was still absorbed in conversation with Grace.

"Our house is really small. So I call it a cottage. I found one of those old metal medicine cabinets in a shed but it's weird inside no matter how I scrub it. There's nowhere to put anything."

Amber's words fell into a lull in the conversation.

Keith said, "Are you whining again?"

Grace said, "Keith. I wanted to— About the doors I found in Shushan," and Keith gave his attention back to Grace. Amber's head hung low, her hands clasped in her lap.

"Amber. Come by sometime," Dinah said, keeping her voice low. "I have a bunch of shelves. Ready-made. They're yours."

Amber nodded and turned away.

Dinah sipped her wine, which was drier than she liked. Her impulsiveness shamed her. She didn't understand why she was here, in this house, in this place. She wanted to be back in Texas. This feeling might be grief or she might feel the same way if Taylor were alive.

After dinner, they trailed into the living room and settled in front of the fire. Grace had found the marble mantelpiece in a shop in Vermont near one of the old quarries; it was carved with fanciful lilies and leaves of ivy. How plain Grace's house used to be, how grand now, adorned with shards from two hundred years of building. Dinah chose the leather armchair. Adler and Keith were talking about the Superbowl. It was snowing again.

John Malcolm took the matching leather armchair before the fire.

He said, "I'm sorry about your husband." He was almost cooing. "It was very sudden?" he asked, and Dinah answered, "Yes. Unexpected. Completely."

Again, the silence of everyone listening. Perhaps at these winter dinners, everyone listened to all the conversations at once to store up human noise.

"Margot had been ill for a long time, as you probably know," John Malcolm said, so naturally that the others resumed their own conversation, or they knew his story already. "But she enjoyed a respite. Then she was back to the hospital. Her only child—from her marriage to Robert Drake, the poet—Leslie had only just arrived when Margot ordered me to the cafeteria. She insisted that I stay away for at least an hour. 'Walk outside, John Malcolm,' she said. 'When you get back, report.' I hadn't stirred from Margot's bedside—I'd slept the night on a glorified armchair. When I returned, she was gone.

"The nurse told me that often happens," he said, gazing into the fire. "The dying often wait until the person they love most, are most attached to, leaves. As if they wouldn't let themselves go otherwise."

Poor daughter. John Malcolm took the title of the best beloved. As if that would make it more bearable that Margot had died without him.

Two doctors agreed that Taylor might have had a split-second awareness of pain or of sudden darkness, but neither physician could say how long a second lasted when blood was flooding your brain. The only sure thing was that he was alone.

"Now the work goes on," John Malcolm said. He was sorting through Margot's unfinished stories, her journal of their rose garden, letters from far and wide. He was her agent, editor, executor, and widower. A collection of the three stories completed in her last year was to be published in a few weeks by a small press that had high hopes for it. John Malcolm was farther along than Dinah in the business of being left behind.

He looked out the window at the gathering snow, stood, and announced that he had to leave, and Amber and Keith sprang up as if he'd given them a signal.

Soon they were gone in a flurry of thanks and promises to do this again. Adler cleared the table, then poured scotch into a short glass while Grace and Dinah started the dishes.

"How did you like John Malcolm?" he asked.

"Sweet. I guess," Dinah answered.

"He makes you feel sorry for him with that stuff about Margot. Women love feeling sorry for a man."

"Margot was fun. Smart. A little pleased with herself," Grace said.

"Maybe she had reason to be. Good night, ladies, good night, good night. I'll leave you to your dissections." And Adler took his glass of whiskey to the study and the late news.

"I invited Amber and Keith at the last minute, but it didn't turn out too badly," Grace said. "She wanted to return my book about vegetable dyes."

"Dyes—?"

"Don't you remember? When I used to crush flowers and roots, boil them? Dunk my crochets and macramés?"

In her young country days, Grace tried her best, as if she had the knack for anything more complicated than sewing a button.

"You need some company," Grace said. "Seriously. You should get a cat. You always wanted one but Taylor's allergies."

"Maybe." Dinah didn't recall ever wanting a cat. She found them beautiful but sneaky.

"When you're ready, we'll find you one. I'm glad you're going to help Amber," Grace said.

"She can take those shelves off my hands."

"She could help. Be your assistant."

"For what, Grace?"

Grace handed Dinah a platter to dry and looked at her meaningfully.

Grace wanted her to undertake some kind of elaborate, expensive, exhausting form of therapy—an antique store, something, anything—but Dinah hated feeling that it might be good for her to get over feeling the way she did, if this was grief, this weight on her.

When the last glass was dried and put away, Dinah looked around for her gloves and car keys.

"Stay," Grace said. "It's snowing. Really."

Dinah didn't want to be lost again in the dark.

As she made her way to the room she always slept in, she told herself not to make a practice of sleeping over at Grace's.

* * *

Dinah was settled in Taylor's chair before the fireplace with a red sketchbook closed on her lap. It was morning.

Taylor had wanted them to have a late adventure, his argument for retiring from his law practice and leaving Texas. They found, at the end of a lane off a back road, the farmhouse and the sentinel maples Taylor required. With the money from the sale of their house in Texas, they paid cash and still had enough left over; enough was a funny concept now that Dinah wanted nothing money could buy.

The snow started again, big dry flakes like feathers from a quilt, very quiet snow. The attention the fire demanded was company for Dinah. The library took its color from Taylor's books and the honey of the pine shelves. For the winter, she'd laid a faded tribal rug; in spring, she'd unroll the sisal rug she was storing upstairs. White wooden shutters hung at the windows, and now they were folded back to show the veil of snow covering the hill.

When Taylor died, he was in the middle of a book of essays by an English psychiatrist, and Dinah had made herself finish the one he hadn't, the one about boredom and solitude.

She'd chided Taylor for building a daytime fire on a cool autumn morning when they didn't strictly need one.

"It'll be warm by eleven," she said.

"We're not in Texas anymore. It won't be warm until May."

What did it matter if he'd burned every stick of wood?

When she got like that, barking orders and objections, Taylor usually looked at her mildly and asked, *Why do you try to control my every movement?* If she'd known he was going to die when he did, would she for thirty-four years of marriage have been a better person? Sense told Dinah, *Sorry, that's not the way it works,* but when she woke and remembered the nauseating fact of his death, she thought, *If I'd only known.*

Dinah knew how to clean a house and put stray objects in piles. She knew where to place the blooming Christmas cactus so that it glowed in the room and lifted the view of snowy hill and stone fence. But she didn't know why she should take the trouble.

In death there was no longer a particular self; the person who had been there was gone. When she found Taylor slumped in his chair before the fire, she knew that his soul had taken off, and now she knew that she was stuck in her particular existence without him. Dinah wished that he would haunt her. Some dead might linger but Taylor was gone.

Is happiness something you will? Her happiness had wrapped itself around Taylor. Making breakfast, reading the papers on Sunday, Dinah would look over at Taylor and realize that she was happy, not ecstatic, not excited, but happy as sunlight sometimes looked happy. There was an element of will in the realization, a forcing of awareness. Happiness was shy and began to retreat as soon as she noticed it. At other times, in the same set of circumstances, she'd been discontent, had glanced over and found Taylor infuriating. At those moments she'd craved something else, though her desire was unreadable then and now.

Sometimes when Taylor was away on a business trip, the change had felt like a holiday for Dinah—silence in the house, slovenly freedom from obligation—but it was a parody of this crushing absence.

Taylor had assumed that they'd have children. When they were first in love, Dinah had assumed it, too. Then Dinah said, "I'm afraid," and Taylor asked, "Afraid of childbirth?" "No, not the act, but—" If they had children, would they lose one another? *No,* Taylor said, *it'll be like more of each other.* Dinah didn't believe him.

For their first decade together, Dinah looked critically at every child she saw, wondering if she could mother such a creature. She turned away from babies, lest one reach for her. Arguments against children were easy. Look how exhausted their friends were, how they had no energy or time for their own lives aside from the children.

Should we have had children? It was easy now to answer, *Yes.* The rock-bottom truth was that once having had Taylor's gaze of love and serious consideration on her, she couldn't share it, not even with their own child. If she had given up her fear, might she have kept him longer?

Her sadness would not bring him back no matter how faithfully she nursed it.

The white snowlight coming through the window covered the gaudy cactus blooms. In the oval mirror above the mantel the light was changing. The wooden frame of the old house fit together like a sailing ship's; it breathed with the wind, the floor joists crackling as Dinah wandered from room to room. She paused by the window in the mudroom and saw that the sky was darkening. The snow was changing to heavy, icy flakes that coated the trees and fences and the bare sticks of the lilac hedge.

Upstairs in the front bedroom with its still-packed boxes, Dinah located the white wire shelves, the labels and price tags intact. She'd carried the shelves eighteen hundred miles. She didn't use them in Texas. What made her think she'd use them here? Though now there was that girl Amber.

The shelves were leaning against the corrugated box of diaries. She didn't remember replacing the box.

She left the shelves where they were and carried the box downstairs, and spread the diaries on the library rug. They smelled of mold and damp.

She opened them, one by one, glancing at the neat penciled entries, catching words here and there. The diarist wrote: *flannel petticoats, chimise, Hiram went up to the Village with a cord of wood.* The writing was so neat and small, and the diarist usually packed the three lines allotted for each day. The entries were recordings after the event. *Basket Quilt. Sprinkling. It has been very warm the Bees have been flying around like summer.*

Dinah arranged the diaries in three rows of nine, from 1874 to 1902. Twenty-seven books for twenty-eight years. The missing year was 1875.

Most of the little books were the same kind, leather-bound, stamped Excelsior on the front cover, with almanacs on the first pages. On the inside, *Mary Ann Rathbun, Easton, Washington County, New York* with variations: *Mrs Mary Ann Rathbun Her Book* and *This Book Has Lots In It.* One black leather diary, 1887, was covered in feathery gray mold. Dinah pressed a finger on it; the mold didn't transfer.

The diaries were made with places to tuck in small remembrances—a letter dated 1902, typewritten and addressed to *Grandma*; a recipe for Pork Cake; an advertisement for Gabler Piano, Cluett & Sons, Troy; an inch square of aqua velvet. Hidden for over a century from light, the color was a secret or a message; here was consideration, desire, intention.

When she looked up, it was almost dark. She returned the diaries to the little box and set it on the library table.

Dinah threw on a jacket and gloves, got into her boots without lacing them, and left the house.

In the corral formed by the barns a fencepost protruded from mounds of snow. On the north side of the big barn, a rusting plow blade and pieces of a tractor waited beneath the snow for her to do something about them.

She slid open the door of the small barn where the car and truck stood like faithful steeds; slipping between them, she climbed up into the cab. It was unlike Taylor to choose such a fancy pickup: room for passengers, leather seats, silver-blue.

"Can't live in the country without a truck," Taylor had said. "Might as well have the one I want."

She couldn't decide what to do about the truck. She might not have to decide. The cost of keeping two vehicles was probably prohibitive.

Nothing in the compartment on the driver's door, and in the navigator's place, state maps, Dinah's spare lipstick, sunglasses, and a traveler's pack of Kleenex. In the glove compartment, a flashlight, roll of Tums, Taylor's sunglasses.

Behind the driver's visor, a plain sealed envelope. Her breath came in clouds and icy tears coated her eyes. She tore open the envelope with her gloved hands. It was a note from their realtor about the title search.

The barn was gloomy and smelled of rusting metal and dripping oil; it was a shop barn, Grace had said. Broken farm machinery rested along the walls. A workbench spanning the back was covered with rusted tools and parts, and cans of oil, its surface stained with WD-40. Dinah reached to set one can aright, then thought better of it. She could make out tools—hammers, screwdrivers of various types and sizes, wrenches rusted beyond moving. There were cans filled with cobwebs, nails, and screws. A vise clamped the rough boards, its jaw rusted shut. Once this was the center of fixing and mending, of keeping the home and farm working. The people kept animals, grazed them, mowed the hay field, considered draining along the road where cattails filled the swamp and a layer of ice formed between the bleached stalks. Once, the top of the work-bench would have changed every day. Now it was a permanent exhibit—Daily Farm Life, Circa Forever—and there it remained, patient and neglected. The barn waited as if its people would return at any minute to take up the tools, oil them, get them clamping and pressing, twisting and pushing again.

Maybe the diaries were under an enchantment, and if Dinah read them through, the workbench would straighten its overturned oil cans and clean its grime. Maybe all the possessions left behind by the suddenly dead would awaken and apologize for outliving their people.

Dinah was in bed when Amber called.

"I was wondering about the shelves? The ones you offered the other night?"

Whining again.

"I'm glad you called. I found them today," Dinah said. "I'll meet you anytime. Weather permitting. At the bakery?"

Amber whispered, "Would you mind if I came to your house?"

Dinah gave directions; Amber seemed eager not to prolong the phone call.

October Thursday 25
Lois put up the Lace Curtains this morning and made the paper
Curtains and
Put them up
And the bed valances
And now we will Call the Parlor and Bedroom done

Lace, like light through snow. White plaster walls and shining woodwork, bull's-eyes at the corners of doors and windows—this house could be Mary Ann Rathbun's. But she didn't know that it was.

The paper in the 1877 diary was flexible. High cotton content. The diarist was a woman sewing, cleaning, cooking, taking care of children. Mary Ann didn't speculate. If she dreamed, she kept it to herself.

If Dinah read the diaries every day, the names and places would become familiar. Day would follow day. Time would pass. She saw herself working on Taylor's computer, transcribing the diaries so everyone could read them. Taylor would have tracked down Mary Ann Rathbun's history and found out why her diaries were in their house.

Good bye old year. So Mary Ann began 1874, the earliest diary. *January 27,* she went with Alta *to see Doctor Langworthy and we got some medicine of Tefft 48cts. February 4: 2 Alta went with her Father to the Doc and got some more medicine and paid him 2 dollars.*

Dinah squinted, held the diary this way and that to shine light on the faint numeral: *2.*

February 1874, Wednesday 11: 3 Kenyon took Alta up to see the Doctor and get some Medicine. it has been a very foggy rainy day.

There were so many names: *Stevie, Annie, Lois, Charlie, HC, Hiram, Lewis, Piney, Alta, Jennie, Eunicy. Kenyon, Kinyon, Kinnie.*

Mary Ann didn't say who anyone was. Mary Ann didn't talk about the future or recall the past. There was only the endless present, nouns and more nouns.

Dinah looked up from the penciled words.

The afternoon was no longer young, though it wasn't yet evening. How vivid and familiar Mary Ann's weather had become: foggy, snowing, rainy days, the themes and variations of winter. The falling snow looked solid now. A white wall was forming around her. What did old people do around here? Didn't winter invade their bones to the marrow? The sky and falling snow whitened; the barns blackened. It was a Japanese woodcut, a farm scene, the ox weighed down by a load of branches, the farmer swathed in blue cloth, and the snow falling in white dots.

The fire was dying. The wind was picking up.

Dinah fetched the ash bucket from the woodshed and shoveled the fireplace ashes and coals into it. On her way through the mudroom, she put on boots and Taylor's barn jacket, hat, and gloves, and carried the bucket to the corral, dumping its contents over the fence onto the waiting snow as if she were feeding slops to a hog. The coals sizzled and gave off a sharp smell. The sky was lowering and the air moist.

Dinah set an armful of logs by the woodstove in the living room. She opened the stove door and heat coated her face. She loaded the stove carefully, closing the vent almost all the way.

Dinah built a new fire in the library, working carefully and slowly. Her skin and hair were saturated with wood smoke. Back in the mudroom, she shed her scarf, gloves, and jacket, and changed back to house shoes. Through the window installed the previous summer she saw their skeletal apple trees only because she knew they were there.

When you've been married a long time you don't think anymore about the other person; his presence is there. Now that she and Taylor were out of touch, Dinah didn't know quite where she was. She wasn't in Washington County, Cambridge Township, she wasn't home in Texas, but in a state of suspension between one and the other.

Being with Taylor had kept the sensation at arm's length but it had always been there.

Dinah waited at the mudroom window. When it was almost dark, a blue Ford pickup stopped at the barn and Amber stepped out, cradling a bundle in her arms. Her red hair was bare to the snow.

"Hello! I didn't know if you'd make it. Leave your boots right there."

Dinah moved from the doorway to let Amber pass.

She hung her down jacket on a vacant peg, pulled off her boots, and slipped on the pair of fuzzy blue slippers Dinah slid toward her (they wore the same size, Dinah noticed). Amber's left cheekbone was smudged, and she wore an indigo-blue sweater, knit in a complicated pattern (it must have cost a fortune). She rubbed her bare hands together to warm them.

"I need to get the truck back to Keith," Amber said.

"The shelves are upstairs," Dinah said. "How about a cup of tea first?"

Dinah chose a white china teapot and dropped in pinches of tea. She opened a package of Scottish shortbread wedges.

"This house is so . . . It's grown-up," Amber said.

"You should have seen our house in Austin. It took a crowbar to get me out of there."

Amber said, "There's so much I want to do but we're broke. Keith tells me to save my energy. We don't know how long we'll stay. This isn't what he expected. He's only been here in summer."

"Me too!" Dinah said. "Everything's better in summer. Longer days. Taylor and I came for the summer forever. Every summer for years and years. Last summer, we moved here."

"I can't think that far ahead," Amber said. "Summer. I love your house. I love Grace's house, too. I brought way too much stuff from the city. I brought everything I own, dumb, dumb, dumb, but there was no one to leave it with. My mother's had it. I don't like to live with stuff half in boxes and half out, like when we need something I have to unpack for it, but I can't just toss it all away." Amber laughed. "I guess."

Dinah thought of the big barn with plenty of space for storage.

"You're in the accumulation stage of life, Amber. I'm at the other end."

The kitchen windows were mirrors as the sky darkened.

"Keith doesn't want us to have anything."

They carried their second cups of tea to the armchairs by the library fire.

"I moved to New York to go to design school. Fashion design, but one thing led to another. I finished two semesters. One and a quarter. I was waitressing when I met Keith—it turned out he knew my brother from the army—and now I'm here. We're here."

Amber stood and looked at herself in the oval mirror above the mantelpiece.

"I left home with my husband. That's when my family gave up on me the first time. He was sweet but he turned into a mean drunk. I supported him. Which is where my tuition went. I worked as a temp, data entry, boring, boring. I left him in the middle of the night because he'd laid hands on me once too often."

She held up her left hand. Her fingernails, painted bronze, glinted in the firelight. The pinky was bent.

"It healed wrong. He kept saying I didn't need to see a doctor." Amber touched her nose, also crooked. "I figured I'd better get out of there while I had a straight bone in my body." She laughed. "But the thing was—I worried how he'd survive without me."

Her joke didn't deserve the laughter she gave it. Dinah wondered what she'd looked like before anyone hurt her.

"And Keith?"

She meant: Is he different? Is he kind?

"Keith wanted to kill him but I'd never tell him Tommy's address. My family doesn't like the way I live. The thing is . . . my mother doesn't like me and she never has liked me," she said, and she laughed again as if it were the silliest thing she'd ever heard. There was a smugness now to her laughter, as if she were pleased with her situation even while seeing how hopeless it was. If Amber were her daughter, Dinah thought, she wouldn't like her to travel from one man to another.

"There's something—" Amber retrieved her bundle from the kitchen and returned to the fireside. She laid the bundle across her lap and began to unwind the swaddling of tissue. "This is what I did at fashion school."

It was a jacket, narrow waisted, buttoned at the navel with a dull stone, lapis lazuli perhaps. The fabric was satin, blue, almost black. It must have been like sewing water.

"Model it!"

"It won't go over this sweater."

The sweater covered Amber from below her ears to above her knees. Dinah realized that Amber had made it herself.

"You put it on," Amber said. Dinah's shoulders were too broad so she draped the jacket over the back of a chair. The garment had such presence that now there were three of them in the library. *Look,* Dinah wanted to tell Taylor. *See? This girl is talented.*

"I'm not original like Keith."

"Not true. What do you really want to do?" Dinah asked. "Make clothes? Sell them?"

"I'm going to put an ad in the *Pennysaver*," Amber said. "Tailoring. Custom sewing. Do people do their own sewing around here?"

"They used to do everything themselves. I don't know about now."

"I can clean houses. I got pretty good at it in New York. It's funny the way it is when you're cleaning someone else's place, like who trusts you and who assumes you're a thief," Amber said. "Keith didn't like it that I was in strangers' houses. He didn't like it when I was waitressing either. Strangers there, too."

Dinah would talk to Grace, who'd know the right places, and Dinah saw herself going to stores in Saratoga, in New York, with the beautiful jacket and the sweater, winning commissions for Amber, saving the day.

It was dark by then.

Dinah went up the stairs first and turned on the lights. Amber was behind her.

"Here," Dinah said. She opened the closet door and retrieved the shelves. Amber reached for them.

The sound of the rising wind drew both women to the window.

"Oh, man," Amber said. "I hate this weather."

The sky opened with bone-rattling thunder, a crack of lightning, then a crash that shook the house.

Dinah handed the shelves to Amber. They rushed downstairs to the mudroom, shoved on boots and jackets, and burst outside.

One of the giant maples was down. It had missed the house, the stone fence, the electric wire.

Amber said, "Your tree."

It lay across the road, its branches still quivering from the fall. They braced themselves against the wind, mesmerized by the proportions of the disaster. The tree was monstrous on the ground.

Amber said, "I have to phone Keith," and ran as if Dinah might stop her.

When Dinah reached the house, Amber was hunched over the phone. She looked at Dinah. "It's too late." She hung up, resigned—and something else, Dinah thought. Afraid.

Dinah telephoned the town garage. They had three emergency crews out. There might not be anyone available before morning.

"That's fine. Put me on the list, please," Dinah said, and told them where she was. They knew the place. They knew the tree.

"We should have some dinner," Dinah said.

Dinah unpacked the refrigerator and began constructing a meal. She hadn't planned to cook, but here was Amber.

"Let me help," Amber said, "please. I want to do something."

The smells and sounds of the cooking made the kitchen come alive.

When they settled at the kitchen table, Amber touched the wood, as if she were memorizing it.

"It's tiger's-eye maple," Dinah explained. "When you slice and polish it, it brings out markings that look like eyes. It's a rare wood."

"Anything could happen. Like this wine." Amber waved her hand over her glass of Zinfandel, its dark color catching the light. Amber's hand stopped, the executioner's axe halted in midair. "Don't you worry?"

"We had a few accidents," Dinah said. "Then we saw places where other people spilled things. We figured we were in a long line of eaters and drinkers and spillers."

After the meal, they washed and dried the dishes, and Amber phoned Keith again.

"He has to be there," Amber said. "Without the truck, he can't get up the hill to the cottage."

He must have known where Amber was; why didn't he phone her?

"I always get him dinner. That's the way he likes it to be. Dinner on the table."

"Maybe the neighbor drove him home," Dinah said. "Try your house."

Dinah's suggestion made it worse.

"Oh, no. I hope not."

"Try the operator, Amber. See if the phone's down."

Amber's face was white when she made her way back to the armchair in front of the fire.

"All the lines are down over there," Amber said.

"I'll bet he got caught at the neighbors', just like you did here."

"I hate not keeping promises," Amber said.

Whatever was bothering Amber, she'd tell Dinah or not. Dinah gave a clean flannel nightgown to Amber. "You'll be cozy in the living room," Dinah said as she led Amber back through the kitchen. Dinah made sure there was wood enough in the living room stove, then turned down the air intake so the stove would burn low through the night. She found sheets and a pillow, an armful of soft blankets, and was preparing to open the couch to make the bed when Amber said, "Just lie the sheets and blanket on top."

"Lay," Dinah corrected automatically. "Like 'Now I lay me down to sleep.'"

"We used to say that at home," Amber said.

"Good night. If you need anything—"

"I'm fine," Amber said. "I won't bother you."

In the middle of the night, Dinah woke to men's voices and lights twirling. She stood shivering at the front window until she realized that it was the snowplow. Unable to pass the fallen tree, the plow retreated, and she returned to sleep, wondering if the noise had disturbed Amber at the back of the house.

Later, in the part of night that never liked to budge, a second crew arrived. Soon came the whine of chain saws.

She threw her clothes on and found Amber in the kitchen, making coffee.

The women carried thermoses and mugs down to the crew and passed among the men, Amber pouring white and black coffee, and Dinah following with sugar. The men talked about the storm and how much worse it was on other roads. One, who wore a home-knit scarf over his jacket, told Dinah, "You're lucky that tree fell the way it did. It would have hit the house good," and another said that up on Kenyon Road, the hay barn was split in half by an elm, one of the few still around. The men kept their eyes on Amber and addressed their remarks to Dinah.

Dinah's tree trunk had fallen across the road, which was town property; they were cutting it up in chunks to move it out of the way quickly. "But we're throwing it on your land," the foreman explained, "so it's yours." He warned her, "Don't burn it for a year." The men threw their cigarettes in the snow and handed back the mugs.

At the kitchen sink, Amber lined up the thermoses and mugs. Dinah said, "I'll do them in the morning."

"I can do it," Amber said. Her face was bright from the cold, and Dinah said, "Go to bed, we'll get it in the morning."

Dinah rearranged herself in bed, curling into the mound of blankets and quilts, lulled into sleep by the sound of chain saws and the chugging of the trucks.

At daylight a fire was crackling in the library, the wood smoke perfuming the morning.

Amber stood at the kitchen window. The kitchen was clean, every surface wiped and shining, the thermoses and mugs dry on the rack. Solitude and orderliness resumed their sway over the landscape. The road was plowed and the snowy fields pristine. The night's drama of the fallen tree, and the dark figures of workers and machines, was ended, leaving the snow in front of the house littered with chunks of wood and the corpse of the giant maple.

The clean kitchen touched Dinah. She'd thought of Amber as someone to give to, and here she was, helping.

"I have to go," Amber said.

"But you'll have something to eat. Eggs, toast—"

"I didn't think you'd mind. I ate already."

"Of course I don't mind. You've been waiting for me to wake up."

"Yes. And—"

Amber was quivering with the need to be gone, yet she waited for Dinah's permission. Amber started to speak, then closed her mouth over her words.

"Amber, what's—" But an intrusion into Amber's privacy might have taken away more than it would give. "Come again soon, please," Dinah amended. "Come anytime. I'd like that."

Amber pulled on her boots in the mudroom and carried the shelves out to Keith's truck. Dinah stood at the doorway, still in her robe and slippers. She wished she'd given Amber more.

The day was especially beautiful in the aftermath of the storm. The sun sparkled on drifts of snow. The barns stood like monuments, as mysterious as sphinxes. While her truck filled the morning air with pale exhaust, Amber brushed last night's snow off the windshield, then, with a wave, she was gone.

May 1874, Sunday 24
It has been very warm
today Hiram and I took
a long walk around the
mountain

June 1874, Saturday 20
Put a oleander to sprout
in a bottle today

July 1874, Thursday 23
They drowed in the first
load of hay today I made Jelly
to day and cannd some
berries and picked some sage

December 1874, Wednesday 2
I finished Lymans
Coat to day
killed the
Pigs to day

Laundry, ironing, quilting, dressmaking, three squares a day, bread and cakes, berrying, canning and pickling, trying lard, making soap and candles.

Dinah wondered where Mary Ann got her oleander and if she knew how poisonous it was.

Both sides of the road were littered with wood, and broken

branches were everywhere. Down, the maple still stood taller than Dinah. The long-buried roots gave off the sharp odor of the deep earth. The peonies, daylilies, and bleeding hearts that bloomed along the stone wall were used to being sheltered and shaded by the tree. They'd be surprised when spring came.

Later, Dinah drove to Saratoga to stock up on wine and cheese. She wandered down Broadway, considering the store windows. Nothing tempted her. She could have anything, needed nothing, and that dampened her itch to buy. She took the Northway in the wrong direction, toward the airport, exiting at the route she and Taylor took when they flew in from Texas. Signs for new subdivisions lined the road. The ice cream stand with its white minaret had vanished. At Stillwater she crossed the Hudson River. In Easton, Dinah turned onto Fly Summit Road, and she swooped over the familiar hills and curves too fast. The fields and woods were full of snow, as though it were a permanent condition. Did Mary Ann Rathbun ever feel a wild yearning to leave this beautiful place, so cultivated and divided, or did the views satisfy her when she looked out from wherever it was that she'd lived? The whole way home, Dinah didn't see another soul except cows and crows.

Grace appeared from the kitchen, holding a dish towel and saying, "Glad it's you. We're not ready. I took a nap and I couldn't wake up."

Adler stood by the dining room table, a drink in one hand, a fistful of silver knives in the other, listening to a Brahms trio playing over the speakers. Tall beeswax candles burned in the silver candlesticks, and their light softened the hard china circles.

"Please, Grace. I can't take it anymore," Adler said.

"What can I do?" Dinah asked. "Don't you like Brahms?"

"The Brahms has been playing all day. I'll give the poor man a break," Grace said. "Sit down and talk to me." Grace was experimenting with Indian food, and the air was mustard colored with odor. Sitar music replaced the Brahms.

Adler poured three glasses of wine, handing one to Grace at the stove. They raised their glasses to one another, then to Dinah, and Adler drifted away.

"Something I thought of today," Grace said. "It's a lucky thing you're here. At this moment in your life." Dinah laughed. "Really. This is the right place for a widow. Easier than at home somehow. In Texas. Now you can—"

Evelyn and Richard Babcock came through the door, with loud, cheerful greetings and cold air clinging to them. They were Grace's friends from the preservation society; together they'd appealed time and again to the planning board to stop trailer parks when farms were sold. Evelyn and Richard collected antique farm implements; Grace had told Dinah that their walls were decorated with ice saws, washboards, and wooden pitchforks. Before retirement, Richard had been a lawyer in the city; a light local practice and volunteer work now occupied his time. He wore his hair in a buzz cut, and with his chest swelling beneath his Aran sweater, Richard had the posture of a military man. Evelyn was pale and gaunt, her fading blond hair gathered in a thin ponytail. She wore black cat's-eye glasses. When Dinah learned that she and Evelyn were the same age, she was surprised, then wondered if anyone else would be.

Evelyn commandeered a reading lamp in the living room and adjusted it for her needlepoint. The light revived Evelyn's hair. Her skin looked lustrous as she bent over the work.

A woman sewing, Dinah thought, *a sacred sight.*

Their oldest grandchild had just been admitted to Cornell, Richard's alma mater, and the talk drifted to grown children. Adler's son was a music producer in L.A., successful at the moment. Grace spoke of taking her favorite niece to lunch in New York last month; the girl was doing beautifully at Lehman Brothers. After lunch they'd gone to Bendel's and bought each other presents.

Richard and Evelyn also lost a big tree in the storm. Theirs was a rare walnut and though they were sorry it was down, they had plans to make a harvest table from its trunk. "We were just in time!"

Richard said. "Thank God!" They'd stopped the road crew from chunking up the noble tree and throwing it on the side of the road.

After the first and second glasses of wine, Adler said, "I guess John Malcolm didn't make it back."

"Oh, he'll be here," Grace said. "He would have called." Still, they began without him, and by the time John Malcolm arrived, they had finished dinner and Dinah was ready to make her excuses and leave.

Evelyn was saying, "I've been after him to come for weeks, and when he finally showed up, it was of course at the wrong time. But I dropped everything. He came to fix a window. It wasn't a big job, mind you, but we're considering some rather extensive changes and we hoped he might do. A nice, steady carpenter. You haven't been through this yet, Dinah, but you'll find it's impossible to get anyone to do decent work."

"No," said Dinah, "I—"

"Well, when Keith's truck pulled up, I jumped, I can tell you, offering him tea, you know, whatever he needed. He's been doing small jobs for us since he moved here. Richard's the lawyer for the estate he and that girl live on. Keith was building us bookcases. Never enough bookcases.

"Well, I was the only one home," Evelyn said. She took off her glasses. Her eyes looked tired. "Richard was in town at his office. I was in my study paying bills, and Keith was in the downstairs guest room at the back of the house. I heard noises. I couldn't quite make them out.

"I went over and saw him stepping on our new kitten with his boot, deliberately hurting the little creature."

Adler laughed. "Oh, Evelyn. Maybe the kitten was in the way."

"Kittens do get underfoot," Grace said.

"I saw it with my own eyes," Evelyn said, "and when Keith realized I was there, he let the poor kitty go. It was sickening. I never want him in my house again."

"You'll have him in your house, woman," Richard announced,

"or learn to build bookcases. He does good work and charges fairly. Keep the animals out of his way."

"Many people have an aversion to cats," Adler said.

John Malcolm seemed to have no opinion about cats, nor any interest in the subject. He'd just returned from a publicity tour for Margot's new book. He'd made an all-out assault on the reading public at bookstores, in classrooms, and on public radio, and announced, "The first printing of Margot's new book sold out."

"Copy by copy from John Malcolm's own hand," Adler said.

"The publisher is very enthusiastic," John Malcolm said.

At a large Midwestern university, John Malcolm had met an assistant professor who'd written her dissertation on Margot's early stories; now she was planning a definitive critical appraisal of Margot's work.

"Isn't it a little soon?" Adler asked.

"Not at all. The first decade after the death of a writer is crucial. You must keep the name alive. Well, that's all settled. Barbara will be here in the spring to look at the archive."

"It must be nice to have an archive," Adler said, "not just uncontrollable piles of paper."

"Margot saw to that," John Malcolm said. "Before she became too weak. She supervised a great bonfire and saved only what she wanted seen."

"Very prudent," Richard said.

"Of course, what she burned is precisely the kind of thing that people want," Adler said. "Not that it matters."

Over dessert, Evelyn turned to Dinah and said, "Grace tells me you're doing so much for that little place of yours."

"The house is almost done. Upstairs needs painting. You might be interested—I found a box of diaries."

"Whose diaries?" Adler asked.

"Mary Ann Rathbun. The diaries go from 1874 to 1902."

"I wonder why they're in your house," Grace said. "Is it a Rathbun house?"

"No doubt a Rathbun house at some point," Richard said.

"Are you sure it isn't Rathbone?" Evelyn asked.

"There are other names on our deed. Cornell. Not Rathbun."

"A mystery," Grace said.

"R-A-T-H-B-U-N?" Richard asked. "I know the name. Can't think where. Give the diaries to the preservation society when you're finished with them."

"Yes!" Evelyn said. "We'll accept any old thing."

"I'm thinking about transcribing them," Dinah said. "So other people can read them. If only the lives of important people survive, then what happens to people like Mary Ann Rathbun? I feel responsible—"

"And curious . . . ," said Adler.

"Yes, nosy," Dinah said. She smiled because he was right.

"Curiosity is a different emotion than nosiness," Evelyn said.

"A history of the ordinary," John Malcolm pronounced.

"You have to ask yourself," Dinah said, "why this busy woman took time every day to pencil sentences, notes, about her life, her family and community. So far as I've read, she mentions the names of over fifteen people, maybe family, maybe working on the farm or neighbors—I can't tell their ages or relation to her, but they're there—and why did she do it?"

"Oh, lots of people kept diaries then," Evelyn said. "It was a fad."

"She was bearing witness," Dinah persisted. "Mary Ann was bearing witness to her life."

"It's a miracle they weren't thrown away," John Malcolm said.

"Maybe she was bored," Adler suggested. "Stuck on a farm with all that virtuous work to do."

"People were far less stuck than they are now," Evelyn said. She began to pack up her handiwork. There used to be a trolley that ran along Railroad Bed, Evelyn told them. It took passengers to town or to connections to bigger places and to any of the little stops along the way. "To the Summit, to the Corners," Dinah said.

People rode horses to get over the fields and roads, or used a wagon or a carriage to get where they wanted to go. Or they walked on their own two feet.

The Babcocks and John Malcolm left, and Adler retired with the eleven o'clock news. Grace and Dinah cleared the empty bottles and glasses and the cloth napkins thrown down carelessly. The saffron stew was glued to the plates; the women set about washing and drying.

"I wish Evelyn wouldn't tell that story everywhere she goes," Grace said. "Keith won't get work if people say things about him. He's new around here, so people don't know what to expect. If Keith had a nasty temper and they'd known him all his life, it would be different. A woman on Scotch Hill Road told me that he was doing some work on her barn, repairing siding that had rotted, and she heard some funny pounding. It was Keith hitting a piece of siding, I mean, whacking it with his hammer. Something about it frightened her. He came to the house later sweet as pie with a fresh Band-Aid on his thumb. He said he'd hit his thumb. Well, I guess he was taking it out on the barn."

"I wonder if he'd do that kind of thing if a man were around," Dinah said.

"Keith's not to my taste," Grace said, "but I like Amber and he's got to earn a living somehow."

"Amber says they moved to the country so he could be serious about his photography."

Grace laughed and clapped her hands together. A spume of soap bubbles rose and fell.

"Women are such suckers," Grace said. "They can't just love a man or have an itch only he can scratch. He has to be a cause."

They dried their hands and made a plan for Grace to go over to Dinah's. In the spring, after Memorial Day, Grace was going to plant a vegetable garden for Dinah. She thought the corral was the best place, since the soil was well fertilized. Grace's choice had advantages: Dinah could see it from the house, it got good sun, and the barn provided shelter for tools and the cart Grace had given Taylor for Christmas.

Town was dark as Dinah passed through. Two houses had porch lights burning.

She didn't go to sleep but poured herself a glass of wine and looked in her photo album, her photo archive, John Malcolm might call it. There, among the snapshots of vacations and family gatherings, Dinah came across a color photo her father had taken in his old age near Plum Creek, where he lived, of a meadow with rain lilies blooming, the little white flowers that appeared after rain, formed three large seeds, then died back. The simple white trumpets shone against the dark trees and scrubby grass. The image went straight to Dinah's heart, the rain lilies standing like brave ghosts. That field, that featureless landscape, was her place, her country. She took the picture from the album and leaned it against the dictionary on the library table.

One evening, Richard Babcock phoned to say that he'd remembered why the Rathbun name sounded familiar.

A family named McCann from the hills off Easton Station Road had come to see him about their house, built in 1836, brick with unusual fan windows. McCann and his wife were from Troy but had lived there for years. Now they were thinking of putting it on the market and wanted Richard's advice. It was a Rathbun house, they said.

She wrote down their phone number on the *Pennysaver* that lay open on the kitchen table, right where she'd left it that morning. Everything stayed where you put it when you lived alone. *For Sale:* Canning jars, a tractor, *still works.* Snow tires with *some wear.* Land and mobile homes and houses. Kittens and puppies were free. Amber hadn't put in an ad offering her services as a seamstress.

It would take forever to finish reading the tiny penciled entries in the diaries, much less recording them.

All her life Dinah had watched and waited. She was a widow, as Grace had pronounced, older, richer; she could help this girl if it pleased her to do so. She remembered waking and finding the coffee made and Amber waiting for her. No one else would lift a finger to help the girl. People almost never did. Dinah could keep Amber occupied, first on the diaries and then lending a hand—curtains, upholstery, and cushions. Dinah's desire to thwart Keith felt a little delightful.

The spiky rain lilies gleamed against the dark grass.

The McCanns' dirt road ran along a ridge near Willard Mountain, which was almost fifteen hundred feet tall, a bump compared to the Rockies but high enough so that a signal from its summit was once visible to the Revolutionary soldiers across the Hudson during the Battle of Saratoga. Taylor had liked that fact; he'd intended to climb someday to the exact spot. The road fit snugly in its niche, overlooking the farms in the valley below.

Mrs. McCann had sounded as if nothing would ever surprise her, as if she got telephone calls from strangers asking for a tour of her house every day. "Come up Railroad Bed to Easton Station Road," she'd said in a low, rich voice. Dinah imagined that she was a large woman.

The McCanns' sprawl of barns and outbuildings was covered with siding broken with age. There was no sign of active farming. The brick house was handsome, its gable end facing the largest barn, the front door facing the road. At the gable, the unusual fan window, as Richard Babcock had described. Beyond the house, a steep hill rose to a scrubby tree line.

At the back door, Dinah knocked, waited, knocked again, and heard a faint, "Come in!"

The yellow-checkered wallpaper in the kitchen was brighter than the day. Mr. and Mrs. McCann sat at an oval table that took up most of the room. The yellow-and-white checked plastic tablecloth was covered with mail and newspapers, toys and seed catalogs. The room felt hot after the chill outside.

Mike stood and offered Dinah his hand. He was a large, gray-haired, blue-eyed Irishman, probably in his late sixties. He held his head tilted to the left, as if he doubted what he was hearing.

Noreen McCann was tiny, with short white hair that expanded from her head in waves, as if animated by her energy. She said, "Hello, hello, we've been expecting you, you said three, well, it's close to three." She made a gesture to Dinah. "Sit down, won't you?"

Dinah took a place opposite them, thanked them for letting her come, and complimented them on the beauty of their view.

"I found some Rathbun diaries," she said at last.

"So Mr. Babcock said." Mike disappeared under the table, emerging with a shoebox bulging with papers. "Mother's work."

"Mike's mother took an interest in local history," Noreen explained. "She pursued it for years. Writing up to Fort Edward."

"Did she meet the Rathbuns?" Dinah asked.

"How old do you think we are?" Noreen asked. Both McCanns laughed.

"There wasn't Rathbuns left to meet," Mike explained. "Not even when my grandpa bought the place. It was my grandpa bought the place from Con O'Brian, and it was Con bought it from Rathbun. *Stephen Rathbun* it says on our deed."

Stevie and Lois up the Excursion to the Hoosac tunnel. *Stephen M. Rathbun, Easton,* written on the back page of a diary.

"My mother's name was O'Brien," Dinah said. "With an 'e.'"

"O'Brian. Con's name," said Mike. "With an 'a.' Help yourself." They watched as Dinah drew the shoebox to her.

"Neighbors," Mike said. "She was interested in where the lines were of the old farms. So far as I remember, the father or grandfather of the Rathbuns, maybe the great-grandfather, owned a thousand acres, which is including the ski area, though it wasn't for skiing in their time."

On the back of an envelope, Mike McCann's mother had traced ownership from Rathbun to O'Brian to McCann.

Dinah took out her notebook and copied down the numbers on the deeds, still in their envelopes from the county office in Fort Edward.

Noreen asked, "Would you care to see the house?"

Dinah pushed away from the table.

"It's a good house. Built in 1836, so far as I know," Mike said, following them. "There's parts that aren't here anymore. Every farmhouse had a washroom. That's gone but there's a lot the same. Brick houses weren't plentiful. The walls outside are three feet thick, you can see that down in the cellar. There's an old part and a new part come together." He pointed to a hump in the floor. "There was a milk room off the kitchen, there where the sink is now."

On the long table at the center of the dining room lay papers and projects begun and abandoned, Christmas decorations, some whole, some in parts. Every surface in the room—tables, chairs, shelves—was covered by boxes bulging with quilt batting, picture wire, plastic flowers, gewgaws.

Noreen and Mike slept in the front room; most of the room was taken up by a bed and piles of knitting magazines and yarn. Dinah glimpsed quickly through its open door before following Noreen upstairs. Mike said his hip was bad and he'd stay below.

Upstairs was unheated, with a cat box in the hall. The house had been hard used for generations. Noreen toured Dinah through the rooms, keeping up a recital of what needed to be done, how she planned to do it, and why she hadn't yet. She meant to replaster the ceilings that were cracked, to paint walls and refinish floors.

"I'm intending to change the wallpaper, all of it," Noreen said, as she already had in the corner bedroom overlooking the barns. She'd steamed off layers and layers of old paper—nasty work—then pasted on the small floral pattern now covering the wall.

"You did a good job," Dinah said.

"Here, on the doors. You see that? That's called graining," said

Noreen. "They had that in the old days. They did it with a comb through the wet shellac."

The trees had grown in the intervening years, more than a century, and changed the light. Nowhere in the house was there an obvious place for Mary Ann's constant sewing. The last upstairs room was the hired man's room, barely big enough for a single bed.

"Do you care to see the attic?" Noreen asked, indicating a door.

"Please," Dinah said.

"We don't go up in winter, as a rule," Noreen said.

"I'd love to see it."

The attic hung duskily between the fan windows at each end. Two massive brick chimneys rose through the roof. Abandoned hair dryers, hot-curl sets, radios, boxes and boxes from the McCann sons and daughters covered the floor. When Dinah was growing up, there was no family clutter; her mother went away when Dinah was a little girl, and after waiting a long while Dinah's father cleared the place of everything she left behind.

"There's nothing of the Rathbuns here," Mrs. McCann volunteered. "It's all ours."

Her children's basketballs remained and their dolls, broken and ruined by the looks of them, but Noreen wouldn't throw them out herself; she wanted her children to sort out their own things themselves.

"I tell them they'll be sorry someday when I'm gone and they have to clean it up all by themselves, and they laugh at me," Noreen said.

"When my father died," Dinah said, "there was just me to empty the house," and Noreen nodded, satisfied.

Downstairs, Dinah gathered her gloves and keys, her notebook with the notes scrawled on it. She was thanking them and thinking of the drive home when Mike McCann asked, his eyes bright, "Don't you want to see your Rathbuns? That's where your Rathbuns are, in the Rathbun burying ground. If you want Rathbuns, that's where you'll find them."

Down the road, back in the direction she'd come from—she'd missed it entirely. High above the grade of the road, barely visible unless you knew it was there, the cemetery looked like trees among more trees; on close inspection, you saw that a black iron fence set apart a rectangular space. The uprights of the fence were shaped in three lozenges: the lowest, half-buried, bulged out at the sides; the middle was a simple egg; and the highest echoed the angle of the bottom, ending in a crude fleur-de-lis. It was once a fence of distinction. Good-size saplings grew among the gravestones. The road bank had been cut so sharply that the near corner of the fence hung in the air; the ground had been scraped away beneath it.

"The county," Noreen said. Each winter the county snowplows took away a little more of the road bank, despite her calls and protests.

It was a scramble for the women to get up to the graveyard. Mike didn't try, citing his bad hip. The gate was held open by clumps of frozen weeds and snow. Noreen McCann made a sound of displeasure.

In one corner were two thick headstones, unornamented except for words incised on top, *Mother* and *Father,* and on the face:

FATHER HIRAM C. RATHBUN 1823–1908. FATHER, HUSBAND, HCR
MARY ANN RUMBOLD 1823–1907
HIS WIFE WEEP NOT THAT . . . GOD GRANT . . . MOTHER

Dinah got down on her hands and knees to read the rest of the epitaph but couldn't make out the words. Mary Ann's stone was sinking or the ground was rising. Acid rain was eating the words. Dinah pushed aside the crusted snow and ice, and the frozen blades of grass beneath, but she couldn't read more than *His Wife Weep not that . . . God Grant . . . Mother.*

Mary Ann had died the year before Hiram. *His Wife.* Born in the same year, they died a year apart. The stones were identical. *Rumbold* was Mary Ann's maiden name.

Dinah took out her notebook.

"Some come in the summer," Noreen said, "to do rubbings. There's older and better stones in the Easton cemetery."

Noreen made her way down to the road and stood shivering. Mike McCann had long since returned to the house.

Lyman
born September 16, 1835
died February 12, 1906
Alta
Died February 11, 1875
18 years 3 months
Daughter of Mary Ann and Hiram
Patience, wife of Paul
Died March 23, 1856
88
Paul
Died March 13, 1848
84

The sun was so far down that she could barely see. Dinah joined Noreen on the road, her fingers clenched with the wet and the cold.

"Did you get the twins?" Noreen asked. "Over in the corner. Twin boys. Babies it looks, from the size of the stones."

Dinah climbed back up to add *Albert and Almont 1864* to her list.

"The graveyard's on our property, trees growing where they shouldn't and the fence in peril, but it isn't mine nor Mike's. We won't be buried there."

Noreen talked about the attic and the graveyard in the same way: tasks that needed doing. Dinah started to offer help cleaning up the graves when spring came, but she was doing her own neglecting; her father's grave went unvisited in the town cemetery in Texas, Taylor's ashes were in a plastic urn under her bed.

It was dark when she drove down the hill to Railroad Bed. She hadn't expected Mary Ann's house to be so substantial and brick. Despite the number of people and the endless domestic demands of keeping them fed, clothed, and healthy, Mary Ann wrote over and over, *We done all we could,* commenting on work that would never be done and gave each day its shape.

"It wasn't just McCann stuff," Dinah told Grace on the phone when she got home. "It looked like there was something from everyone who's been there since 1836. There had to be Rathbun things."

"You'll never know. Or not on the first visit. I'm amazed they took you around. Maybe they think you'll buy it."

"That poor woman. She'll never clean the place up and you can see it growing every year, boxes from every Christmas present—"

"It's the clutter of history around here," Grace said. "It overwhelms people so they can't deal with it. And they can't appreciate the history either because they're held hostage by it. They don't know what to do with it."

"Now I know when Mary Ann lived and died. Who she was married to. Hiram. When he lived and died. That's the H she walked around the mountain with, her husband."

After they hung up their phones, Dinah heard the silence of the house around her. She thought of calling Amber but it was late, and besides, she didn't have the enthusiasm right then.

Dinah thought of the graveyard high up in the dark, trees rustling.

At daybreak, the hedgerow was covered with hoarfrost. The ice changed prismatically when the light met it, giving the familiar trees and hills an enchanted aspect.

The strange light fell on the bedroom walls and the faded Chinese rug and polished floorboards. Everything in the room was in harmony. Nothing looked new or set in place for effect, as if Dinah had been there always.

Her cross-country skis had waited since the snowless November afternoon when Taylor hung them in the mudroom. Dinah laced her boots, pushed open the door against a fat drift, attached her skis, and slid into the world.

Toward the barn, one foot, one foot, making her way uphill to the big barn, where she stood panting. Snow mounded over the fallen maple. The pink Christmas cactus blossoming on the library table was the only color and sign of life.

Past the barn, past the invisible property line, into the ice-covered woods. No one else, no tracks or imprints of skis or snow-shoes. There were signs of subtle creatures: gentle indentations of bird feet and deep slender holes where something four legged had plunged into the snow, a deer or one of the dogs from Fly Summit that wandered looking for trouble.

Up the logging trail, all new territory. Taylor had told her about a magnificent view that he'd reached at the height of autumn color, but she didn't recall his directions. Shuffle and glide, poking along, breathing hard; she was warmer than she'd been since she left Texas. Taylor's sweater was too heavy. She took it off and tied it around her waist.

Her little house was still in view, the barns standing companionably nearby, a small nation-state. Dinah pushed on, glancing back until she saw it no more.

What if she fell, what if she couldn't get up? Who would miss her? Who would seek her? She'd left tracks but who would follow them? The sun was up. The hoarfrost was disappearing. The trail ended but Dinah continued vaguely east until she came to a stone fence, forgotten and still intact. She'd thought of winter in black and white, now she saw color; each stone was its own country, contoured and varied, wet black to persimmon orange. The snow held color in blue shadows and black hillocks. The soaked and furrowed tree bark was full of its own busy life, housing insects and moss. A bird streaked by so fast that it disintegrated, only part of it leaving for the unknown.

Dinah pulled off her glove and scooped up virgin snow, pressing it to her face until her skin was burning cold.

The stone fence was the outer border of communal existence, beyond it wide open spaces, someone else's land—too steep for haying—and the woods. The fallen snow, her breath visible before her, everything radiated life.

A crow screamed. There was alarm in that cry, as if a dreadful discovery had been made. She retreated past maple and rock, fallen pines, until a group of buildings lay ahead, barns and a house. Before she recognized her home, she envied the owner.

The volunteer at the counter was a dumpling of a woman with gray braids coiled about her head. She greeted each customer by name, and they embarked on a detailed discussion of family and the fickleness of the weather, skipping the January thaw and leaving them with so much snow. Her long skirt swept the floor as she filled paper bags, weighing and marking them, talking all the time. How lucky Dinah was that her hair had turned silver rather than that dull shade of gray. The Co-op was long ago the opera house, with concerts and performances upstairs. There had been a store here even in Mary Ann Rathbun's time; now it sold organic grains and pure dairy products, local goat cheese, wooden toys, pottery, weavings.

The customer at the head of the unruly line was ordering from a long list, a quarter of a pound of this, three cups of that, exclaiming in annoyance when the Co-op didn't have what she wanted, wondering if her item shouldn't be ordered, then ordering, which required the slow filling out of more pieces of paper.

Dinah wanted her breakfast cereal and short brown rice, and she wanted to leave. She gave up her place in line and wandered into the next room, a gallery for local artists. Black-and-white photographs hung framed on the long walls. The air was cooler in the empty room. A banner: KEITH WRIGHT. In the dim winter light,

Dinah moved close to the photographs: white china vase, Volkswagen Beetle, steel bucket filled with water. Keith's subject was the moment just before spilling, tripping, falling, the paralytic moment when you see what is happening and can't prevent it. Inevitability lingered in the photos. The VW will hit the telephone pole, the vase fall from the shelf, the water's integrity crack when the bucket is lifted. Amber's hand moving over the glass of red wine. Dinah wanted an image of Taylor before the aneurysm burst, the quiet room, his intelligent mind taking in sentences about boredom and solitude.

Overhead lights came on.

Keith stood in the open doorway, his blunt hand resting on the switch.

"They look better in the light," he said.

He looked smaller than the first time they'd met but more powerful.

"They're remarkable," she said. "You should have lots of success with these."

"Nothing's sold," Keith said. He smiled as if failure helped him win a bet.

"They're full of tension. Violence," she said.

"So I hear." Keith glanced around. "The crowd's thinning out. Are you finished looking?"

She wanted to buy a photograph to thwart his sureness.

He turned out the lights and followed her to the line of customers.

"Amber got home all right after the storm?"

He nodded.

Dinah said, "I've been thinking about Amber—"

Suddenly they were at the front of the line. The woman in braids greeted Dinah with the bare politeness given to strangers and let her eyes flicker over Keith; she went into the back room to measure out Dinah's cereal and rice. Dinah heard a voice close to her ear: "Leave her alone—"

Dinah stepped backward and bumped into Keith.

"Sorry," she said.

He nodded. "Your order."

The lady with the braids was waiting for Dinah to pay.

"Amber? It's Dinah. I may have a job for you. Well, you might not want it. Transcribing some old diaries I found. Don't worry. I have a laptop I can let you use. No, I'd be happy to come and how else can we do it if you don't have a car? No. No trouble at all. Tomorrow? If tomorrow's okay with you, it's fine with me."

It was done.

Dinah was cooking, a glass of red wine on the counter nearby, the news beaming human noise, and she glanced at the glowing light from the fire in the library. The next day Grace was leaving for New York, going in for a haircut and a facial, appointments with her dentist and doctor. She'd be gone for two days, but tonight she was coming over for dinner. A light snow was falling; it seemed to Dinah that it had little heart. How much more snow could fall, how many more white mornings? How much longer could winter last?

The phone rang and startled her.

"I'm not going to come over. I need to get organized to get to the city and things piled up. Sorry. What did you do today?"

Dinah told her about the Co-op and seeing Keith.

"He warned me."

"Are you sure?" Grace asked.

"No. I'm not sure. I'm not even sure it was Keith—I heard someone say something."

"Nothing ever happens to me when I go to the Co-op," Grace said. "Come with me to the city? That's one of the reasons you moved here."

"I'm the one who didn't want to move here, remember?"

"You can get your hair cut."

"You're tempting me," Dinah said. She'd taken to wearing a black velvet ribbon around her head; after an hour, the ribbon slipped and the hair escaped. "Next time. Drive safely. Take care of yourself."

Grace laughed.

"That's all I do, in case you haven't noticed."

Dinah sliced and minced and chopped as if Taylor were waiting to enjoy the food, as if Grace were coming. At home, even if she did little in a day but clean out drawers or file papers, often she'd resented breaking off to make dinner for Taylor. She loved and resented his return to the well-kept house on their cliff in Austin; she'd appreciated and begrudged the nourishing food she made for him. No one would ever do the same for her.

She shouldn't have said that Keith's work was violent. How condescending and insincere she must have sounded. Yet it was true. The images were nothing she wanted to see every day, nothing she wanted in the house.

When Taylor was alive there was a world of things she could say only to Grace and not to Taylor; now that he was dead, she noticed the many things she never said to Grace. She was curator of her marriage, collector of swift moments and unremarked-upon sensations.

After dinner, she made tea and in the library reordered the little diaries for Amber. In the last days of 1874 and on the Memorandum and Account pages:

Mr Willie Sprague and
Mifs Jennie M Rathbun
Was Married the 3d of Jan

The quilts and dresses were made for Jennie's wedding.

Ella Tucker stayed from January 2 to 4, 1875. Perhaps Ella was a cook or hired girl come for the wedding. Jennie Rathbun must have been Mary Ann's daughter, Alta's sister.

January 8, Alta knit Lewis a pair of socks and he left for Indiana.

January 13, *Children have had the Chicken Pox.*

The last entry for January was in another hand, a signature, *Stephen M. Rathbun, Easton.* Stephen Rathbun who sold his family's house to Con O'Brian when he was an old man.

In February, Lewis left again, this time for Connecticut. He was the wanderer.

On February 9, it was ten below zero.

Three weeks after the chicken pox:

> *The Children have got the Whooping Cough*
> *Doct Hults was here*
> *To see Alta today Feb 10 the first*
> *Time*

> *Richard Herrington Died*
> *Feb the 11 and was buried the 16 1875*

> *The 18 of feb Jennie come*
> *Home and staid until*
> *The 21*

> *The 19 I put on a horrick*
> *Plaster*

The tenth of February the doctor came to the house to see Alta.

She checked the graveyard list in her notebook. Mother. Father. Daughter. *Alta Died February 11, 1875. 18 years 3 months. Daughter of Mary Ann and Hiram.* Mary Ann didn't write, *Alta died today.* She didn't write, *She looked peaceful* or note the weather when her daughter was buried.

The grave down the road to be visited. The other children to take care of. The life of the family and the farm rushing on past the dead girl. She wouldn't record the date. Mary Ann believed that she would never forget it.

The children's chicken pox and whooping cough finished Alta.

Count the times you had the doctor.

With the tiny numbers next to the entries about Alta in the 1874 diary, Mary Ann was numbering the progress of Alta's decline—Alta who had been ill the whole year, perhaps longer, perhaps for years, Alta who used up precious cash for the doctor and the medicine made in town, who needed care at home and didn't pull her weight in the work of the farm, and so Mary Ann had traced her daughter's every ordinary action, her candlemaking and sewing, her purchases in town. And when Alta died, Mary Ann must have wondered, *How could this have happened? Did we do everything we could? What did we miss?*

Child-sized stones in the family cemetery. Loss wasn't new except each time. *Albert and Almont 1864. Annie Sophia. October 14, 1865. 16 years, 7 months, 3 days. Alta S. Died February 11, 1875. 18 years 3 months.*

Jennie, newly married, came back home to comfort her mother after Alta's death.

Count the minutes you had her.

Did you do all you could?

Driving Taylor's truck gave Dinah a high view of the road. At the bakery, she bought a bag of fresh crullers; the smell of warm sugar and grease filled the cab. By her side was Taylor's laptop and the box of diaries; she was keeping 1874, but the rest were for Amber to transcribe.

A few miles south of town, a road uphill toward the national forest. It was a rough road with few houses along the way. Rocks rose through the snow, and saplings and full-grown trees splintered the fields; it had been a long time since the fields were cultivated. Past a weather-beaten farmhouse, once yellow.

The diaries had survived long neglect but she wondered how safe they would be at the end of this road.

All unknown roads seem long. The truck could turn upside down in a snowbank. *You entertain yourself with disaster,* Taylor said.

Dinah had imagined Keith's house as a rectangle made of Lincoln Logs, but it was a white bungalow that wouldn't have been out of place in Austin. Probably built in the 1920s, L-shaped, two stories with a high-peaked roof, a porch with fancy trim. The paint was peeling. The windows and storm door were covered with plastic for the winter. The pines around the house were broad and forbidding. Even on a sunny day, the house would be in their shadow.

Amber appeared as soon as Dinah pulled in.

"I'm so glad to see you! I was afraid that my directions were wrong," she said.

"Am I late?"

"Here. Let me help. Please."

Amber carried Taylor's laptop, Dinah the crullers and box of diaries, up the path to the porch. Amber shifted the laptop to her left hand and reached for the doorknob, turning back to Dinah, then caught sight of the white bakery bag.

"The bag," she said. "He'll know you were here. He'll see the bag."

"I brought plenty," Dinah said.

"He won't be back until after dark. He'll know you came when he wasn't here."

"The laptop? The diaries? Amber, I don't want to make trouble for you. Maybe—"

"He doesn't object to me earning money," Amber said. "He wouldn't like me socializing."

Inside, Dinah took off her jacket and scarf, dropped them on a chair by the door with her gloves and hat.

The house was larger than it looked from outside. Downstairs, the walls had been torn down, leaving an open room and bearing columns with wires hanging from them. There was a steep staircase, almost a ladder, at the center. The only walls enclosed Keith's dark-

room. Amber showed every corner of the place to Dinah. A green
enamel woodstove heated the open space. Keith's work covered the
walls. The floor was painted gray. In the kitchen area, gilded and
painted plates from Occupied Japan hung in a wide arc over the
stove and old-fashioned refrigerator. A weathered table and four
chairs served as the dining room. Two white slipcovered armchairs
and a worn blue rug made up the living room. Amber had sewn
cushion covers for the armchairs from quilts and quilt covers; the
cushions were piped in black.

Their bed was made of logs, high off the floor, and charming
as an illustration in a children's story—*Little Red Riding Hood*. A
white cat with a red collar was curled on the bed, sleeping.

"Mavis," Amber said. "My kitty-cat."

The peaceful, picturesque bed reminded Dinah that you never
know what goes on between lovers. She knew nothing about Amber
or Keith. None of this was her business.

"Your house is like *Little House on the Prairie*," Dinah said, and
Amber's face bloomed into a smile.

"That was my favorite book ever. I loved it when they had in-
fluenza and she was crawling across the floor for the water bucket."

"And the water spills," Dinah said. "The girl never gets a drop."

Amber led Dinah upstairs. "Keith made me a special little place
up here. In the spring, he's building a better staircase. Be careful.
This one's cobbled together."

Halfway up the narrow stairs, Amber reached back for the laptop. Amber reappeared and Dinah handed her the box of diaries.

At the top of the uncertain stairs was a workroom with Amber's
sewing machine and cutting table, her scissors and threads, cloth
and ribbons neatly stored. Around the edge were wooden trunks
and stacks of boxes with quilts draped over them.

They set the computer and the diaries on a table in the corner;
Amber reassured Dinah that she knew how to use the laptop and
would be careful with the diaries. She showed Dinah a black velvet
tube filled with beans, which she'd made to hold the diaries open

without breaking the binding. From the diamond-shaped window, a blaze of sunshine fell on Amber. On her left cheekbone was a shadow or a bruise. Amber's wrists stuck out of her cardigan, fading yellow bruises on them. Amber cocked her chin and said, "Keith made all these cubbies for me. It's the first time I ever had a place for all my junk."

Downstairs, Amber made tea and put the crullers out for them to share. She licked the sticky icing from her fingers and said, "I'm getting my sister to send me some cotton gloves. She works in a museum and they've got tons of them. That way I won't touch the diaries at all."

"What happened to your face, Amber?"

The girl's fingers went straight to the bruise.

"It was a mistake," she said.

"And your wrists?" Dinah asked gently.

"It isn't like you think," she said. "You don't know me. I was a mess until I met Keith. He straightened me out."

In the spring, she said, at Easter, she and Keith were going to stay at his family's place on the Cape. He wanted them to get married.

Dinah thought that she could make Amber leave, such a passive and malleable girl.

"Amber, you know. You can always come to me for—help, shelter, anything. I'm serious."

She could support Amber, help her through college or whatever she wanted.

Or perhaps there was no problem at all, except in Dinah's mind. There was an explanation for everything.

Dinah said, "Think about it. And forgive me if I'm speaking out of turn."

"I'll have the diaries transcribed so fast it'll make your head spin," Amber said.

"Leave all of her spellings," Dinah said. "Keep the lines just the way they are."

At the door, Amber handed Dinah the bakery bag with the crullers, and she waited on the porch as Dinah started the truck. Mavis appeared beside Amber and licked a white paw thoughtfully.

In the rearview mirror, Dinah saw Amber waving at her, standing in the cold much longer than necessary.

Grace called the next afternoon from New York, and Dinah told her what she'd discovered.

"She wrote down the number of stitches for socks but not her daughter's death. A neighbor's death but not Alta's. The most feeling she shows is about the weather. *Rain rain rain right straight down.* One Sunday *it was a long lonesome day.* She made a note when Mr. Quackenbush came to do the graining on the doors, you know? And five days later when he was finished."

"Just because she didn't write it down, doesn't mean she wasn't feeling grief. People up there are like that," Grace said. "They talk about facts and the things that happen. Everyday things. That's why it's such a relief to be with them."

"Maybe you're right."

"I'm wearing myself down here. All this maintenance." She'd been to her dentist and doctor, had her hair cut and colored, facial, manicure, pedicure, massage. She'd made appointments for Dinah for the next trip.

In Texas Dinah had been busy every day, making meals and caring for the house, driving along Austin's streets and highways. She had things to do for Taylor, small, repetitive tasks—*Pick up clean shirts.* She saw friends and went to classes at the university every few semesters. Everything in her life had called her to respond to it. Here, nothing needed her. Each day passed. Day and night moved along. Only she was unmoving. Nothing was continuous without Taylor.

The pile of wood and the debris of the giant maple still lay under the snow in front of the house. In another time or place, she'd have seen to it by now.

She wished she kept a diary but couldn't bring herself to start one. A diary of daily life, one like Mary Ann's, demanded notice of fleeing time; an interest in living might grow from such attention.

In a year she wouldn't feel the same sharp loss. Mechanically, biologically, it would happen without her volition or participation, like a broken limb mending. She wanted nothing more to change and everything to change.

Taylor's brother Charles was calling again. The first few weeks after the death he called and then he stopped. Now he called and told her how much everyone loved her and missed her, and asked when she was coming home.

Home!

She'd called the Babcocks one afternoon, and Richard said he'd asked around in the Easton Historical Society for her. The town clerk had given him something that might be useful for Dinah. One of these days he'd get it to her.

As if to reassure Dinah that winter wasn't over, snow began to fall. It had been a week or more since she'd heard from Amber.

The noon sun cut through the hanging blooms on the Christmas cactus. Dinah let the phone ring twenty times. After an hour, Dinah telephoned again. Amber answered after two rings, and Dinah told her that she wanted to take her to the cemetery at the Rathbun farm. Now that she knew the Rathbuns a little.

"I don't have any way of going anywhere. Unless I walk, and that takes a long time."

"I'll come get you," Dinah said.

"Pick me up at the bottom of the road?"

"I'll drive all the way up, door-to-door service," Dinah offered, but Amber said, "No, no. You leave in an hour, I'm sure we'll get to the road at the same time."

Dinah pulled up at the drive-through window at the bank, withdrew cash from her savings account, and parked in front of the Co-op while she separated the money into different envelopes, writing on one.

Amber stood on the shoulder of Route 22, small against the eighteen-wheelers churning their way to Vermont and Canada.

"Did you wait long?" Dinah asked. Amber's face and ears glowed stiffly from the cold.

"Uh-uh. I walked down and just got here pretty much right now." She laughed. "When I really get cold I turn blue. When I lived in the city, I used to freeze at bus stops. The air here is so dry and clean. Wow. This truck." She took off her glove and rested her bare hand on the leather seat.

"Look in the glove compartment," Dinah said, and Amber reached in and pulled out the envelope with her name written on it. "It's an advance. I didn't know how many hours you worked, so you figure it out and next time you can give me a tally. I thought cash would be easier than you trying to cash a check." And cash is easier to hide. She'd given Amber a lot, leaving it to Amber to guess that Dinah was saying, *Leave! Leave now while you can,* giving her enough money that she'd have a chance to start another life. No one had ever said to Dinah, *Take a chance.* And she never had.

"Thank you," Amber said. Dinah waited for her to open the envelope and say, *Oh, it's too much,* but she tucked the envelope in her jacket pocket. When they were in town, Amber said, "Isn't it amazing how different you feel when you have a little money in your pocket?"

They stopped at the bakery. The cab of the truck filled with the smells of sugar, coffee, and cardboard. Dinah felt like she was playing hooky. They could drive to Saratoga Springs, find a good restaurant. They could do whatever they wanted. The truck was bounding down the hills to the flatness of Railroad Bed.

"Sometimes it looks so perfect here," Amber said.

"When we go by the Rathbun cemetery," Dinah said, "I don't think I want us to stop. I don't want to bother the McCanns. They don't own the graveyard but it's on their property. Richard said they might be selling and I don't want them to think I'm interested."

Amber nodded and set her cup carefully into the holder.

"My mother called," Amber said. "She invited me over when Keith and I go for Easter to his family."

"That sounds nice."

"Keith isn't a hundred percent. She doesn't like Keith. My brother doesn't like him either. Fine with me, I told them. Don't live with him."

"The house." They were almost there. "The McCann house. It was hers. Hiram's brother Lyman lived somewhere nearby with their mother. They're all in the cemetery."

On Easton Station Road, the mountain began. Dinah slowed the truck to a crawl at the Rathbun burying ground.

"Here it is," Dinah said. Amber rolled down the window. The sun blasted through a crack in the oncoming evening. For a moment the cemetery was lit orange; the iron fence looked strong and new, black against the orange snow. The light shifted. The derelict graves grew sepia, the pale saplings imprisoned behind the tilting fence. Now the sky was complicated. A storm tonight, Dinah thought.

"Where's Mary Ann?" Amber asked.

"Next to Hiram. In the far corner on the left. Mother. Father. Lyman's in front of them. Alta's close to the gate. Let me know if Mary Ann mentions her. Get out and look?"

Dinah watched Amber scramble up the bank. She waited and thought about joining her but before she could Amber had climbed back into the truck.

Amber put her seat belt on, and Dinah started down the road, driving slowly past the brick house. No cars or trucks in the driveway. No McCanns to see her at the graveyard.

"The diaries are boring but they're interesting," Amber said. "Sometimes when I'm transcribing it's like I can see the people, like when you're falling asleep in school."

"Mary Ann wore glasses," Dinah said. "Hiram bought her a new pair in Cambridge and they went back to exchange them because they pinched."

"Of course she wears glasses, with all her sewing and darning and mending. All those stockings she knit for everyone."

The road descended into the valley. At the stop sign at Railroad Bed, Dinah said, "How about you keep the truck? While you're typing the diaries. So you're not stuck."

"This truck?" Amber asked. "I couldn't. You don't know me. This truck's almost *new.*"

"It's not safe for you to be in that house all day with no way to get away. What if something happens and you need help? And the telephone goes. All you have is your cat. Really," said Dinah. "And I'm thinking that in the spring I might start a business. Grace's friends are always ripping their houses to shreds. I could help them, and you could help me, Amber."

"How could I help you?"

"Sewing. Upholstering. Painting. That kind of thing."

"God," Amber said.

"Borrowing the truck doesn't mean you have to. Something better might come along."

Taylor's brother called just after Amber left. Dinah started telling him about the truck, but he didn't want to talk about Taylor's truck. Charles urged her to close up the house and come home. "We all love you so much," he said. "It's no good you being up there by yourself." She told him, as she had before, that she wouldn't leave until the house was finished. All that remained was painting the upstairs. He said, as he always did, "You know best but don't tarry too long."

When their conversation ended, she went up the narrow stairs. The walls were sanded smooth and prepared for painting. All the worst work was done. One summer during college—she'd returned to Texas after her one year at college in the East—Dinah worked as a painter for a contractor who did fast and dirty work for landlords. She could do this. She could choose the colors, those yellows and greens she'd been thinking of months before, and she could paint the walls; when the house was finished she could leave it or stay.

More easily than she could have imagined, she turned around and drove back into town, bought the paint and the necessary equipment, and hauled it back home, missing Taylor's truck. You do need a truck when you live in the country. She used a tacky cloth to get the dust from the walls and the ceiling, and began. One color, like a pale yellow silk, had won against all the others. Ceilings flat, walls eggshell, trim enamel.

At the end of a few hours, the light was gone. Her back, ribs, and arms ached from the work, her neck hurt, but she was glad.

A few days later, when she returned from the walk she'd taken as a break from painting, Dinah found a manila envelope on her kitchen table.

> *Here's a genealogy that a local man prepared. His wife was a kind of a Kenyon and it's of the whole Kenyon line. The Rathbuns are here. Evelyn wants to know if you'd be interested in attending a meeting of the historical society next month. We're having a speaker from the university in Albany. "Domestic Bliss: Catherine Beecher and the American Woman's Home." Look in the Greenwich town library for newspaper reports. Obituaries can be helpful.*
>
> *Yrs, Richard*

Dinah fed the fire and settled with the genealogy before her.

In 1790, Nathaniel Kenyon, a Quaker, moved west from Rhode Island to New York State. Two generations later, Hiram's father owned three farms.

Mary Ann was the daughter of William Rumbold and Mary

Woodhouse. When she was eight Mary Ann came to America from England.

In 1874, Mary Ann was fifty-one years old and had borne sixteen children.

There was an entry for each child, those who lived to adulthood and those who'd died before they could marry and multiply. The children had scattered to the winds.

"They're all here," Dinah said aloud.

In a footnote for Mary Ann's entry: "Since becoming feeble and the husband blind, had lived among their children, who had faithfully cared for them."

So that was what waited after the diaries: the progress of Hiram's blindness, the sale of their farm to their son Stephen, then journeying like Lear and his fool from house to house. Maybe the children were truly faithful and caring. The house, this house, was owned by one of Mary Ann's children, Annie, who'd married Alfred Cornell. The Cornell house went to Annie's daughter. When the house was sold, the diaries stayed behind.

It has been a long lonesome day, Mary Ann wrote on the last day of April 1874, *cold and cloudy, and tonight it is snowing. The grass is white.*

By the 1830s, Dinah's people and Taylor's had left Tennessee for Texas. This wasn't Dinah's country. She was baffled by the beauty of the old farms set perfectly on their skeleton hills, holding fast the secret of endurance, of a life like Mary Ann Rathbun's, filled with ordinary accomplishments and disappointments, the death of children, neighbors, relatives coexisting with the promise that nothing would change.

The phone rang ten times; just as Dinah was about to give up, Amber answered.

"Can't talk."

"How about the morning?" Dinah suggested. "Nine at the bakery?"

"Fine," Amber said.

"You're sure? I could come get you."

When the call ended, Dinah returned to the 1874 diary. She was examining it, not reading it, and found a pocket she hadn't noticed before. She slid her finger inside and found a white card in red ink. The type was hand-set and uneven.

> *The Swan*
> *This is a noble bird in size,*
> *And very graceful in water.*
> *Some think he is vain—*
> *Which is a hateful vice in us.*

Below the words, a print of a swan emerging from dark branches low over the water. Four cygnets followed the mother swan; the ripples in the water were carefully engraved. On the back in faded pencil: *Alta S. Rathbun, Card presented to her by her teacher M. Ware 1867.*

Who was Dinah to judge the quality of Mary Ann's remembrance?

Ten by the wall clock, a newspaper covering the table, Dinah waited for Amber in the bakery. She'd eaten a cruller and used artificial creamer in her coffee. A landscape dotted with dairy cows and they served fake creamer and she used it. An oil truck passed by.

Maybe something had happened to the girl, to Taylor's truck, maybe she'd called after Dinah left the house, maybe anything and maybe nothing. Waiting and still, breathing the sugary air, watching the old men in the corner nurse their cups of coffee, Dinah tried to read the paper. No ordinary waiting, waiting for someone who wouldn't come.

The snow was thickening. Back home, Dinah reached for the phone and dialed Amber's number. There was no answer.

Dinah telephoned Grace and told her about calling Amber and waiting at the bakery.

"Be careful," Grace said. "People are never grateful for anyone messing around in their marriages."

Mike and Noreen McCann were outside in the falling snow, jackets flung over their shoulders as if they were checking on something in the driveway. They waved and she waved back.

"We were hoping you'd get our message," Noreen said. "I have something to show you."

"Come in," Mike said, leading the way to the brick house.

Noreen brought Dinah to a bedroom she hadn't seen before; it had a fireplace and views of the barns and the road. The wallpaper looked new, blue with a pattern of silver fleurs-de-lis.

"I found this," Noreen said, "among Mike's mother's things. After you left."

"Noreen made the frame herself," Mike said. "It's about this house."

Set on the mantelpiece, a public notice: *Vendue of the brick house and possessions of Lyman Rathbun,* April 1906. A month after Lyman's death. Lyman was childless. None of Mary Ann's sons or daughters had wanted the place, so it went up at public auction. April 1906. One year before Mary Ann died, two years before Hiram. The McCann house, the house Dinah stood in, was Lyman's, not Mary Ann's.

"It's on my list," she said. When Noreen looked puzzled, she added, "Of words I didn't know from the diary. *Vendue.*"

"Don't you know that word?" Noreen smiled. "It means 'a sale.' 'An auction.'"

"Of course," Dinah said. "*Vendre.* The French word. 'To sell.'"

"People still say it."

"Well," Dinah said. "I should have reached this conclusion. From other things. Clues."

"What conclusion?" Noreen asked.

"This house was never Hiram Rathbun's. It was Lyman's," Dinah said.

"That's right," Mike said. "The man who bought this place was Lyman's hired hand, O'Brian, and he's the one sold to my grand-dad. Why would you think it was Hiram's?"

"Because— Is there another house? Hiram's?"

"There used to be a house up the mountain," Mike said. "I thought you already knew about that one."

"No," Dinah said. She tried to laugh. "I don't know. The Rath-bun farms—"

"I thought I told you. I could swear I told you. Look. There's a road just past the graveyard, back the way you come," he said, turning her by the shoulder and pointing out the window. "You follow it up, you'll find where the house was. It burned down in the 1940s. Don't recall the year. The war was on, I know that much. I was in high school but I come up weekends to give Grandpa a hand. That house was owned by a man named Con-neley. Liam Conneley. His three children were at home. Daugh-ters. A kerosene stove fell over and the kerosene went everywhere. Well, everyone used kerosene back then, which don't make it safe but there it is.

"The fire department come from Greenwich but the pumper was missing a part and by the time the part was got from town— someone drove down—the house was gone."

"Were the children hurt?" Dinah asked.

"Nope," Mike said. "No one hurt. They must have run like heck to get out of there."

"So there's nothing left."

"I wouldn't say that. The corn crib was still up when I was last there. Of course, you don't know what's happened since. The house foundation's there somewhere. I wouldn't try the road just yet. That car of yours'd never make it. I used to take the truck up but not for years. Not since my hip started on me. It's a wet road, springs in parts of it. The man that owns the land now, he's planted trees up there. Larches for quick profit."

It was snowing still, lazy wet end-of-winter snow. Dinah wanted nothing more than to be back in her farmhouse.

It was all lost: place, house, burned, gone. Mary Ann was only in the diaries.

Why hadn't they told her when she first visited, when she first saw the cemetery, why hadn't they told her that their brick house was Lyman's, that the house on the hill had burned?

She had no claim on their attention or their friendship. They knew nothing about her; they didn't have to invite her into their house. So kind. Not their fault. Dinah's mistake, not theirs. The McCanns didn't care whose house it had been. It was their house, not a Rathbun house.

"Imagine," Dinah said. "*Vendue.*"

They walked Dinah to her car. In her rearview mirror, she saw them standing and watching.

Past the graveyard, there was a clearing in the trees and a slight declivity in the land, where Mike McCann said the road was to Mary Ann and Hiram's farm. A stone fence traced the way uphill. The snow was untouched. The hill was impassable until spring.

Instead of driving straight home, Dinah headed to Greenwich. The library, a new building, was on a quiet side street with a pair of ancient oaks at the curb. Past the glass doors, a bulletin board was covered with notices of church meetings, sales, pleas of *Help Wanted* on curled pieces of paper, testimony to the interconnected life of the place.

The newspaper morgue was in a small back room and preserved on microfilm from the beginning of time. Dinah found them by death date.

Wednesday morning, after a four-day illness from bronchial pneumonia, Mary Ann Rumbold, wife of Hiram Rathbun, quietly fell asleep at the advanced age of 84 years at the home of her daughter, Mrs. Charles Dixson. She was born Feb. 17th, 1823, in London of English parents and came to this country when a child.

Hiram C. Rathbun, whose death occurred at the home of his youngest daughter, Mrs. Alfred Cornell, Wednesday, March 4th, at the age of 85 years was born in the town of Easton June 29th, 1823. Mr. Rathbun was a prosperous farmer until feeble health and blindness overtook him, for the past ten years he was entirely bereft of sight. Mrs. Rathbun died on April 3rd, 1907. Mr. Rathbun's life was passed on the farm where he was born with the exception of 10 years in the town of Cambridge. Both Mr. and Mrs. Rathbun are buried in the lot on the homestead where the family all lie together.

DRIVEN BY DISEASE TO END HIS LIFE.
Lyman Rathbun, a Prosperous Farmer, Commits Suicide.
BROODED OVER INCURABLE MALADY.
Despondency Over Physical Condition Believed to Have Unbalanced His Mind—Opened Arteries with a Razor—Funeral Held Today

The community was shocked Monday to learn of the death by his own hand of Lyman Rathbun, a prosperous farmer who lived near Archdale. Mr. Rathbun, who had been in failing health for a year or two, had become despondent over his condition and it is believed his mind became unbalanced from brooding over his health. The act was committed by opening the arteries in his wrists.

Lyman's funeral was announced, also the burial to follow in the family lot on the Rathbun farm.

Dinah had wondered if her father would kill himself in his last year. She and Taylor hired a woman from town, a Seventh-Day Adventist, who took care of him during the day. Taylor installed phones in every room in case anything should happen at night and had an alarm system hooked up to the police and EMS. Dinah drove out twice a week from Austin. Her father had always been lean; toward the end, his skin was paper thin.

Until his final week, he made his way daily to the garden, to see what it was doing without him.

Dinah had waited for her father to divulge the secret of their lives: that her mother had written to him, begging for news of Dinah, begging to be taken back. Or why her mother had left. Dinah searched through his papers after he was dead and found no trace of her mother.

Once home, Dinah went upstairs; she'd left the room neat and ready for the next day's painting. The color she'd chosen was beautiful in the failing light. The farmhouse was becoming what Taylor had wanted, the perfect shell for their life together.

Downstairs again, she dialed Amber's number.

"Hello?" Amber answered. She was almost whispering.

Dinah decided not to mention waiting at the bakery.

"Amber?" Dinah asked, forcing herself to speak in a normal tone and to keep her voice even. "Amber, I've found out so much. Mary Ann never lived there in the brick house. She lived way up the hill past the graveyard. But her house burned down. The hill's impassable until spring. Unless we want to get the truck stuck. Would you walk up there with me? In the spring?"

"There's supposed to be a storm tonight. Keith says. Remember the night I stayed at your house?"

"I enjoyed that," Dinah said cautiously.

"I love your house," Amber said.

"I've been painting the upstairs. It's almost finished." And then, "There's a room up there you could have." Dinah listened to the passage of air over the miles between them.

"I've got to go," Amber said at last, her voice loud now. "Look. You can't call me anymore, Dinah."

"I could be there in twenty minutes. Do you want me to come get you?"

"I have to hang up."

"Let me know— Let me know—" Dinah said, but the line was dead.

Dinah turned on the radio. It was true, a storm was heading down from Canada with all the chaos of seasonal change.

When Dinah woke in the night and tried to turn on her bedside light to see what time it was, the power was out. Dinah considered moving to the couch in front of the woodstove but stayed where she was. She woke again at dawn. The electricity came back on at seven. When she made her bed, Dinah noticed that there was snow on the floor, blown up from under the skirting, up through the floorboards. She swept it into the dustpan and dropped it in the garbage.

There was nothing to fear, Dinah thought. The storm was over and nothing had happened. Things came out of nowhere, unexpectedly, and you learned to live with them. She could not shake a feeling of dismay.

Dinah dialed Amber's number. Whatever else was going on in Amber's life, this was not the time for her to have the responsibility for antique documents. She would tell Amber that she was coming for the diaries and the computer. While the phone rang, Dinah concentrated on her memory of driving away from the cottage. She saw Amber standing and watching. Amber's white cat next to her, watching also. The cat and the auburn-headed girl, waiting for Dinah.

The morning sun was brilliant, the light broken by shadows from ancient trees along the way. The bare ground showed in patches through the snow. Soon, when the fields were dry enough, the farmers would begin spring plowing. There was something warm inside the air today, the way there was something cold inside the air at the end of August. In town, the proud houses passed and the neglected ones, the yellow brick bank with its new digital clock and the feed store by the railroad tracks, the Co-op, the bakery, the post office.

After the silver highway, the dirt road climbed uphill past the old farmhouses and their barns. The fields were defined by dilapidated stone fences, though trees had long since regained the land. Snow possessed the woods, in banks and drifts, and the tree trunks looked stern. It was more like mountain country than farmland. Though the trees weren't first growth they were tall with thick trunks.

The road stayed rough, and her car felt dangerously low passing over the deep winter ruts. At last, Dinah spotted the house, and she parked next to the trucks, Taylor's and Keith's. Snow covered the path to the front door. No footsteps marred its surface. The woodpile was covered with a bright blue tarp. No smoke from the metal chimney pipe. The lights were on inside.

She knocked on the front door and waited to hear a voice or movement, but there was nothing. She knocked again. A crow screamed and flew through the woods.

She called, "Hello? Hello? It's Dinah." She knocked on the door once more, thought of giving up and driving home, and stepped to the front window. It was hard to see through the thick plastic stapled over the window frame, but she made out what she knew was there: table, stove, refrigerator. She thought, *Oh, they're painting, too. They're painting their appliances red.*

Keith sat in a ladderback chair, his head down on the table. One arm hung still, empty-handed; the other rested on the back of his head. His right leg was placed in front of the left like a sprinter at the starting block. *How tired he must be,* Dinah thought, *to sleep that way.* Taylor's laptop, the little box of diaries, keys to the truck, and the envelope of money were at the center of the table.

Amber was sitting with her back propped against the red refrigerator. She faced Keith as if they were in the middle of a conversation and she'd sunk to the floor and stayed there to keep talking. One leg was straight in front of her, the other bent to the side.

Dinah saw them as clearly as if the window had broken open. She started to run, slipped on the icy porch, and righted herself. She was afraid to stay at the window, as if the window was to be feared, not what she saw through it. She breathed hard and moved back up to the door, forcing her hand to the knob. She couldn't make herself turn the knob.

Back in the car, she intended to put the key in the ignition. Her throat was very dry and her head ached. She sucked in air and used all her strength to turn the key in the ignition until the engine broke the quiet. Dinah put her head down on the steering wheel. Tears cut trails down her cheeks, hot, as if they had been waiting for this moment.

Late in the day, Dinah was allowed to go home. One of the state troopers offered her a ride but she was all right, she told him, and as long as she kept going very slowly this was true. At home, she put the car away carefully, just so, then hurried from the barn's gloom into the last light of day. She walked the path to the house and took off her jacket, sat down and took off her boots. She slid her feet into her house slippers.

Dinah thought about tea, water falling from the kettle, steam rising from a cup, the scent of the leaves in hot water. She splashed brandy into a juice glass and sipped at it. The dark liquid burned her throat and warmed the edges of her iciness.

Dinah sat on her bed, her head down. She wished she could move but her eyes stayed on whatever she happened to see, now the floorboards beneath her feet, now her feet in their slippers. *Lie down,* she told herself, *lie down.*

A week later, the state police returned Taylor's truck, the laptop, and the box of diaries. When they were gone, she searched Taylor's truck, in the glove compartment and under the seat, behind the sun visors, for a message from Amber.

Back in the house, Dinah spread out the diaries on the library table.

Souvenirs of Mary Ann—the advertisement card for Gabler Piano, Cluett & Sons, Troy, illustrated by a lady in a white dress and holding a pink parasol; a recipe for French Pickle—nothing of Amber's.

Dinah started up the laptop. According to the date on the file, Amber had gotten as far as 1881 a week before she died. The trooper said that Amber's fingers were broken. Dinah scrolled through the transcription but the words were all Mary Ann's. She turned off the laptop and put the diaries back in the corrugated box. She moved to her chair in front of the fire.

One, they met at Grace's.

Two, Amber came to get the white wire shelves and stayed the night when the storm knocked over the maple.

Three, Dinah took the diaries and the laptop to Amber at the cottage.

Four, they drove to the Rathbun graveyard and Dinah gave her the money and the truck.

They talked on the phone four times—Amber had called about the shelves; Dinah called to give Amber the diaries; they'd made the date to meet at the bakery; Dinah had spoken to Amber the night she died.

That was all.

The morning after the maple tree fell, Amber was standing at the kitchen window. Amber had started to say something and changed her mind. Dinah had offered her shelter any time she wanted it. Amber might not have believed that Dinah meant it. Dinah hadn't been forceful enough. What would Dinah have done with Amber if she'd landed half-broken on her doorstep?

Something, Dinah thought. She would have done something. But never enough. She was frozen, as she had always been. What she'd disliked in herself at a younger age now had to be accepted. She had never loved anyone enough. She was incapable of it. She didn't know how to do what other people knew from instinct or from the example of their upbringing. She'd spent her life outside, even outside Taylor, peering at other people, trying to guess what she should do next.

A few days after the truck was returned, Dinah drove it to town, thinking during the ride that the time had come to get rid of it. In the Co-op, she spotted Richard Babcock, whose law office was in a neat brick building next door, and he invited her for coffee across the street at the King Bakery.

"Is this the same family as King Road?" Dinah asked.

"Part of the same family. They stopped farming about twenty years ago and now this is their business. They've held on to their land and a fine Federal house. All their outbuildings are in splendid condition. Unusually so."

"Good for them," Dinah said.

"I heard from Amber's mother," Richard said a little stiffly. "I'm the lawyer for the estate Amber and Keith were living on. The owner, Sam, is in Europe and the incident took place on that property, so naturally—"

"What did Amber's mother have to say?" she asked.

"She's devastated, of course. She knew only a fraction of what was going on. I take it that Amber didn't really let anyone in on the full story. But they were very close. They talked on the phone nearly every day. In a way I think that makes it easier for Amber's mother."

"But still impossible."

"Well, yes. It's impossible for any mother to endure the death of a child. Amber wanted her to come visit here in early spring. There was some family connection to this area and she and Amber were planning to track it down together. It was hard for her to get away."

"You know, Richard, Amber confided in me. She told me she was estranged from her mother."

Richard finished his coffee and grouped the heavy mug carefully with the salt and pepper, the glass sugar dispenser at the edge of the table.

"Amber lied to you. She lied to her mother. She had her reasons, no doubt. There's no mystery. You were kind to Amber. You tried. More than most did."

Kindness, Dinah thought as she drove home. *Regret. Disappointment.* Richard had a gift for naming what was hard to bear.

It's been a long lonesome day, she thought, and she wished for the comfort of Mary Ann Rathbun's nameless world.

One morning Dinah awakened to the sound of an airplane hovering low. When she stepped out the front door, her bare feet on the cold wooden step, she looked for the source of the hum. The maple was covered with tiny flowers, and the flowers were dark with honeybees. She didn't know that maple trees flowered.

Nor had she known that there was a bed of lilies of the valley, come early in spring, in the shady place along the stone wall. She had seen real lilies of the valley only once before, wired into a wedding bouquet. Her mother had a round compact with enamel lilies of the valley on top. Dinah hadn't thought of the compact for years; her mother must have taken it with her.

She hired some kids from neighboring farms to clean up the lawn where the maple had fallen. The woodworker who was making the harvest table for the Babcocks out of their fallen walnut came for Dinah's maple. There were pieces that could be made into a small desk for Dinah's office upstairs.

The storm windows were down and stored in the big barn. The window screens were in place, and Dinah opened all the upstairs windows. She was unpacking the last boxes from Texas: summer dresses, extra sheets, a set of dishes she'd forgotten about and would give away.

Taylor's brother Charles would be the first of the visitors from Texas who'd made plans to visit her while they were east to go to the Vineyard or Nantucket or Tanglewood or Glimmerglass. Before Charles arrived, there was Grace's party to welcome John Malcolm's summer guest, Barbara, who would dive into Margot's archive, and perhaps into John Malcolm's life, or so Grace guessed. Charles's room was ready. Decanter and water glass, an extra blanket on the pine chest at the foot of the bed, reading light in place, fresh note-book and pencil in the drawer of the bedside table, a novel and birding book at hand. She wished someone were there to see the room as she did.

Every day in the new season, Dinah discovered the outside of the house; often in the evenings she walked its perimeter, admiring the white siding and black-green shutters, the way the kitchen win-dows reflected the sunset and the apple orchard in bloom, and how nobly the pillars on the side porch held up the angled roof. There were peonies in the bed along the stone fence, their leaves deep green, their buds formed. A bleeding heart grew from a crack in a stone, and Dinah visited the blooming plant each day to admire its rich pink flowers. She thought of the other springs when she'd come to Washington County to rent a summer house. The flowers were a blur outside the windows of her rented car.

The phone rang and Dinah ran downstairs. It was Grace.

"Dinah. Did I ask you to do bread for Saturday? I have it writ-ten down here to tell you—*Bread, Dinah.*"

"I have it written down too," Dinah said, checking in her new appointment book by the phone. "I'm buying it in Saratoga. You don't expect me to bake it, do you?"

"Don't be silly. What are you doing now?"

"Still unpacking. It looks beautiful upstairs. Let me know if you need anything else. Since I'm going to Saratoga anyway."

"I think I've got it. Adler's looking after the wine. It's going to be fine."

From the upstairs window, Dinah saw her hedgerow of lilacs, all the lilacs she could ever want, a fortune in lilacs, each pyramid of blooms hers.

Without the sighing and clicking of the furnace, with the screens in place and windows open, the only sounds in the house were the trees exercising their leaves, the birds singing, the occasional passing car or calling cow, and the refrigerator in its eternal cycle.

The last box had been opened and resealed; maybe Taylor had been looking for something. In the box was a bundle with a piece of white paper folded on top, with Dinah's name in unfamiliar handwriting:

Dear Dinah, I hope you don't mind. I'll be back for it. Amber

A piece of crazy quilt was wrapped around Amber's jacket. The satin looked like water at night, dark with a silver overlay as though it were reflecting a starry sky.

It was easy to imagine Amber alone in the early hours, knowing what she was returning to, unwilling to risk the jacket as she risked herself. Or she might have returned to the house sometime when Dinah was out.

Dinah held the jacket before her and waved it slowly until the arms hung down straight. She hugged it to her, then straightened it again, refolded and rewrapped it in the quilting. She lined the pine chest in the guest room with white tissue paper and left the bundle there.

Early on the morning of Grace's party, Dinah gets into the truck and drives away from her house, her window open to the faintly medicinal smell of lilacs.

She passes the familiar stops along Railroad Bed until she reaches Easton Station Road, where she turns up the steep dirt road. At the Rathbun burying ground, green stalks cover the bank where orange tiger lilies will bloom all summer. One birch shines among the saplings. At the road she'd last seen covered in snow, a stone fence is exposed, down to the ground. In between tire tracks, wet green grass fights with dandelions for the patchy sun. Dinah parks the truck by the road and starts to walk uphill.

Grapevines tangle with other vines and thorny plants, and they cover gleaming stones. The persistence of the stones is remarkable, the fence remaining beneath the busy brambles, wild grapevines, and small white wildflowers, the stones in the dry wall piled up with nothing to hold them for over a hundred years but gravity, balance, and one another. It's unlikely that a garden remains near the house. Mary Ann's wandering years began in 1896. Any number of gardens could have been planted and disappeared since Mary Ann's time.

The stone fence guides her up the long hill. Looking back, hoping to see the graveyard, she makes out the roof of the McCanns'—of Lyman's—house. The mountain is to the north. In the moment when the first Kenyon Rathbun owned more than a thousand acres, the mountain, Hiram's wooden house, Lyman's brick one, it was a family kingdom, and it has gone by.

At the end of the stone fence, a plantation of skinny larches grows in regular rows, tall, mournful, reminders of every song ever sung about lonesome pines and lost love.

The road dwindles to a path. A small building leans away from it. It might be the corncrib Mike McCann mentioned but it's fallen in on itself so that she can't be sure. A field rolls over the next hill. Anything might appear over the crest of such a hill.

No one in the world knows where she is. The thought isn't terrible, only a recognition of solitude, her almost-familiar companion.

Beyond the field, the woods. Up ahead, a barn.

If it ever was painted, she can't tell. The boards are weathered, silver when the sun catches in them. It's a hay barn, storage and feed above and shelter for animals below. Dinah walks up the rough grassy rise and rolls the great doors apart.

The hayloft has the busy quiet of a cathedral. Light enters in streaks through knotholes and falls on mounds of hay and a rusted-out tractor, rake, and seeding machine. These are of recent vintage, long past Rathbun time, but the pulleys hanging from the ceiling have the eternal dignity of the Stations of the Cross, of a life that once was vibrant and now is a story to be told. The barn is dry despite the spring rains.

In the sunlight again, Dinah doesn't know where to look. According to Mike McCann, Mary Ann Rathbun's house was as big as Lyman's. It burned down decades ago, plenty of time for the woods to take over.

The house would have been across from the barn. When her eyes grow used to the woods, Dinah spots a pair of great maples. She crosses the grass-grown path and passes between the trees.

A crowd of berry bushes is loaded with white blossoms. *In the summer,* Dinah thinks, *I'll come back for the berries.*

Dinah peers into the woods, seeking a difference in tree heights, anything to indicate the existence of a structure. *You can't miss it,* Mike McCann said, but he hasn't been up here for years. The berry bushes and other undergrowth are thick. None of the other trees are as old as the maples. She listens to the sound of the wind in the field and woods, the birds going about their business, then the ghost of a shape appears. She pushes toward it through bushes and saplings, keeping her arms raised over her head to protect herself from the thorns.

She stops just in time. Mary Ann's house lies at her feet. It's an open pit, a stone foundation. That's all that's left.

Dinah paces it at twenty-seven feet wide and thirty-six long. At the southern end, three steps climb into the air, to what might have been the kitchen. A small springhouse stands just past Mary Ann's house.

At the north end, broken steps descend. A stone wall has been built inside the foundation, east to west, perhaps to support the weight of a central staircase. Near the wall, a broken brick lies half in the earth, an old one marked *Troy,* and another brick of a kind she's never seen; it looks handmade. Hiram's grandfather came in the late eighteenth century, so possibly the brick is from his time, kept in the cellar just in case. The brick is cold to the touch. Dinah spots a blue canning jar broken and half-buried in the earth floor.

There's modern litter on the ground, too: rusted cans, beer bottles, jar tops—nothing to do with the Rathbuns and the life they made here. Dinah goes up the steps to a place at the edge of the cellar. She's standing in the clearing where the woods weren't able to grow and Mary Ann's house was preserved.

Here, Mary Ann sewed infinite garments and linen. She bore sixteen children, buried some, and raised the rest. She cooked, baked, cleaned. She planted seeds for flowers and vegetables. She gathered and canned food to keep her family alive in the seasons when nothing grew. These ephemeral activities occupied every minute of her life. Here is the mother who stayed.

Now there's nothing left of Mary Ann but the diaries and the witness they bear, the diaries in which Mary Ann never asks the meaning of her work and life.

Still, it's possible to form a picture of a woman who lives and dies with her husband's constant companionship, cared for at the end by the children for whom she'd cared. It's possible that this picture is a true one, and that our picture of Dinah, standing alone at the edge of a ruin, is also true.

Credits for
Previously Published Stories

Several of the stories in this collection appeared previously in the journals listed below.

"The Blue Wall"
Epoch (January 2011)

"The Blue Birds Come Today"
The American Scholar (Winter 2010)

"The Eye"
Yale Review (January 2009)

"A Thousand Words"
Epoch (Summer 2008)

"Here It Was, November"
Subtropics (Winter/Spring 2007)

"Plum Creek"
The American Scholar (Spring 2007)

"The Thief"
Antioch Review (Summer 2006)

"The Right Place for a Widow," a partial and previous version of
"The Mother Who Stayed"
Southwest Review (Winter 2003)

About the Author

Laura Furman was born in New York, and educated in New York City public schools and at Bennington College. Her first story appeared in *The New Yorker* in 1976, and since then her work has appeared in many magazines, including *The Yale Review, Southwest Review, Ploughshares,* and *The American Scholar.* Her books include three collections of short stories, two novels, and a memoir. She is the recipient of fellowships from the New York State Council on the Arts, the Dobie Paisano Project, the Guggenheim Foundation, and the National Endowment for the Arts. She has received grants of residency at Yaddo in Saratoga Springs, N.Y., and in 2009 she was a visiting artist at the American Academy in Rome. She taught for many years in the Department of English of the University of Texas at Austin. Series editor of *The PEN/O. Henry Prize Stories* since 2002, Furman selects the twenty winning stories each year.

THE MOTHER WHO STAYED

LAURA FURMAN

Reading Group Guide
Author Q&A

ABOUT THIS GUIDE

The following reading group guide and author interview are
intended to help you find interesting and rewarding approaches
to your reading of *The Mother Who Stayed*. We hope this enhances
your enjoyment and appreciation of the book.

INTRODUCTION

Written in concerto-inspired form, *The Mother Who Stayed* by Laura Furman moves its readers through three trios of short stories. Each trio concerns a different set of characters whose lives are connected through family, location, or sheer coincidence. Furman's characters run the gamut of motherhood: a substitute mother who discovers that there is no self without the love of another, a motherless daughter who must come to her own epiphanies about the transience of life, and a childless mother who tries to act on her maternal instincts. *The Mother Who Stayed* is both a meditation on and a celebration of domestic American life, spanning generations of women.

DISCUSSION QUESTIONS

1. In "The Eye," the opening story of *The Mother Who Stayed*, several events take place at the Ziegelmans' Fourth of July picnic which serve as a window into the secrets shared by the families in attendance. What are those secrets? Rachel Cantor is a witness to some of the events. How does her new knowledge affect her? What does Rachel's encounter with the fallen maple tree in the aftermath of the storm suggest about the character?

2. "And why didn't the two families get together in the city? One family on the West Side, one on the East Side, both in the nine-

ties. They could walk across the park but they didn't" (p. 26). How would you characterize the class differences between the Ziegelmans and the Cantors? In what way are these distinctions less important in the country, as depicted in "The Eye," than in the city, as in "The Hospital Room"? How do the characters change in the course of the trio?

3. In "The Thief," Rachel Cantor is accused of stealing a pearl necklace from her friend's apartment. "I could see my hand setting the pearls back on Caitlin's mother's vanity. . . . But at that moment I wondered, and sometimes I still do, if I did take the pearls" (44). What motivation might Rachel have had for stealing? Who else might have stolen the pearls?

4. In "A Thousand Words," Sandra, the narrator, revisits the history of her relationship with Marian Foster Todd, an eccentric and beautiful writer. Sandra considers Marian's possible affair with her husband, Per, without ever concluding that it actually occurred. Does Sandra believe that there was an affair? How does Sandra's preparation of her thousand-word prose piece contribute to the dissolution of her friendship with Marian?

5. The narrator of "Here It Was, November" says of her illness: "I might have pressed down to feel the tumor. . . . Still, I felt no desire to know its shape or to probe its private life" (69). How does the narrator's lack of curiosity about her own physical decline compare to her absorbing interest in completing her biography of Marian Foster Todd? What does the narrator's literary detective work suggest about the true nature of Marian's relationship with Dorothea Browne? How does this knowledge change the narrator's ambitions about her own scholarly work?

6. How would you describe Marian Foster Todd based on her characterization in the three stories in the second trio of *The*

Mother Who Stayed—"A Thousand Words," "Here It Was, November," and "The Blue Wall"? How does her character evolve over the course of the trio? What does Marian's late-in-life relationship with Dorothea reveal about her seductiveness and her capacity for duplicity? Why does Dorothea take care of Marian? Did Marian change Dorothea?

7. What do the details of everyday domestic life in "The Blue Birds Come Today" reveal about Mary Ann Rathbun, a nineteenth-century American mother living in upstate New York? Does the "The Blue Birds Come Today" differ from the other stories in this collection in terms of its narrative, time frame, and plot? If "The Blue Birds Come Today" is based on actual events, what makes it fiction?

8. In "Plum Creek," how does Dinah's early loss of her mother—first through abandonment, and later through death—affect her as a child? What do the storm scenes in "Plum Creek" and "The Mother Who Stayed" reveal about Dinah's fortitude and her self-reliance? What does Dinah have in common with Amber?

9. Dinah pursues her friendship with Amber even after Keith warns her to stay away. What is compelling and attractive to Dinah about the friendship? Given that she suspects Keith of physically abusing Amber, why doesn't Dinah do more to protect the younger woman? Do you think she should hold herself responsible for the tragic consequences? Dinah comes to the following conclusion: "What she'd disliked in herself at a younger age now had to be accepted. She had never loved anyone enough" (189). Do you think this is true?

10. How did the unique structure of this story collection impact your experience as a reader? How did the links between the stories in each trio deepen your understanding of the characters?

How did you arrive at the concerto form for this collection?

I was intrigued by the idea of a story having a separate existence, and then another life when it's read along with others. In music, a theme appears and changes. The variations replicate and complicate. They introduce their own concerns. The resolution doesn't negate the emotions raised by what's gone before; rather, it provides a place for the emotions to rest. The movements seem independent—sometimes, movements are played on the radio as individual pieces—but they also exist as part of a whole.

For me at least, reading any type of fiction involves the same recognition, connection, and memory as when I listen to music. The reader of the trios in *The Mother Who Stayed* can move through time, accompanied by the past, anticipating what might come, and understanding each story's singular world while making crucial connections to the other stories.

What are some of the pleasures and challenges of writing stories that are in dialogue with one another?

Short stories are sometimes called *slices of life,* which has always seemed contradictory for works that are complete in themselves. Even so, when I read short stories, I often wonder about the characters, major and minor, beyond the story's borders. A novel satisfies this itch because the chapters reach into one another, and we understand the world of the novel piece by piece over time and through memory. The self-sufficiency of short stories is their challenge and their beauty, but I wanted something else for this book of stories. The challenge of the trios in *The Mother Who Stayed* was keeping the individual stories whole and at the same time allowing them to reach past themselves.

Have you always seen each trio of stories as discrete from the others? At any point were you tempted to "connect" the trios

by having characters from the different trios encounter each other?

That's an interesting idea, but I never considered a larger grouping. The characters are from different worlds. Instead, I sought to make connections among the stories in each trio without compromising the integrity of each individual work.

Art and literature play a predominant role in *The Mother Who Stayed*. What purpose does that serve in this collection? What shared characteristics do artists and writers have that make them compelling subjects?

The ways in which artists and writers differ from others and are the same intrigue me. What is the difference, for example, between Marian and Mary Ann Rathbun? Both characters write. But for Marian, the work comes first. For Mary Ann Rathbun, her work within the family is primary. She stays faithful to those moments when she is writing the diary, but it isn't her most pressing concern. It's a question of self-definition and also of what we value. The stories gave me the chance to explore such shadings of difference and similarity.

Is the larger-than-life character, Marian Foster Todd, inspired by a real-life literary figure or group of figures?

At a certain point, I began to read biographies more often than novels. My reading was uncritical; I wanted to be educated in the world of the biographical subject, whoever it was, and I wanted to follow the twists and turns the life took. Fidelity to facts isn't important in writing fiction, but it's crucial to biography. Yet facts are chosen, isolated, played up or down to make the case for the biographer's point of view about the subject. It all seemed very familiar to me as a writer and as a person. I create biographies about the people in my own life, deciding which details of background or history are telling, which episodes important and which minor, and how the facts add up to a person.

Beyond what I've learned from biographies about the lives of others, I've learned from life that there are people who have an idea about themselves and their importance. The rest of us are figures in the background. The fictional Marion Foster Todd is such a person. The middle trio in *The Mother Who Stayed* revolves around the lives of Marion's minor characters—minor to Marian, that is.

Your collection focuses on mothers and daughters. What draws you as a fiction writer to these relationships?
You might say that the relationship has been my life's study. My mother died when I was young, and the relationship between mother and daughter always drew me because it was one I didn't have as an adolescent and an adult. Once I was a mother myself, my world grew larger, as did my understanding of my own mother and the demands of being a mother. For a writer, there's always a balance to be maintained between what is known and what is imagined. The stories in *The Mother Who Stayed* were written with that balance in mind. I try not to confine my characters to my life.

You found the diaries of Mary Ann Rathbun that are included in *The Mother Who Stayed* in a house in New York State where you once lived. Can you talk a bit about that discovery?
In 1972, when I was beginning to write, I moved from New York City to upstate New York. Eventually, I bought a mid-nineteenth-century house, nine acres of land, and a few outbuildings. The place was a mess, full of broken furniture and junk. In the course of cleaning, I found twenty-three little books, some with paper covers, others leather or canvas. They were almanac diaries from 1874 to 1902, and all the entries were written in the same hand, mostly in pencil, a few lines per day. I was too impatient to give them more than a cursory reading. The phrase *I done what I could* was repeated on almost every page.

In the five years I lived in the house, I came to appreciate *I done what I could*. Occasionally I returned to the diaries. When I tried to match the terse mentions of fields, barns, and orchard to my property, they didn't fit. *Mary Ann Rathbun* was written on the flyleaf of each diary. Some place names and family names mentioned were familiar, though the name *Rathbun* was not.

Ten years later, I sold the house and carried the diaries with me to Texas. Nearly ten years after that, I began to transcribe them. By this time I too was a wife and mother. Most domestic lives are filled with repetitious activities similar to Mary Ann Rathbun's; certainly mine is. As I read the diaries I remembered the double nature of rural stasis—beauty and boredom. My original impatience was replaced by curiosity and a sense that in removing the diaries from their original place, by asserting my accidental ownership of them, I had taken them on as an obligation.

My persistent question about the diaries was, *Why did she write them at all?* There was a late-nineteenth-century fad for diary-keeping but fads are usually dropped long before a year has passed. Yet she kept writing. The diaries seemed in no way written to be read. If Mary Ann Rathbun had intended them for a reader, she would have identified the people she named in relation to herself, as daughters, sons, husband, neighbors; she would have identified herself. As a storyteller, she would have told her reader how she came to be where she was, and why and how she stayed. But she wasn't a storyteller. Her diaries are a private document.

The products of Mary Ann Rathbun's long, hard domestic work wouldn't last—food is eaten, a clean house becomes dirty, in time clothes and quilts decay or are discarded—but by recording the dailiness Mary Ann created something permanent. Her writing was an act of concentration that today we might see as meditative.

What Mary Ann Rathbun accomplished in writing her diaries, perhaps for no one and with nothing more in mind than noting each day as it passed, is an embodiment of her time and place.

In "The Blue Birds Come Today," you depict nineteenth-century American domestic life. How challenging was it to inhabit

that era fictionally? To what extent did Mary Ann Rathbun's diaries enable you to do so?

The diaries gave me lots of mysterious clues and information I had to interpret. My time living in upstate New York gave me feelings and some knowledge of the countryside and the life there, but it took a long time, many years, for me to find a way, as I did in "The Blue Birds Come Today" and in "The Mother Who Stayed," both to break away from Mary Ann's literal life and to honor it in fiction. Through much experimentation and rewriting, I was finally able to transform all that material—the diaries, landscape, memories, and emotions—into art. When I finished "The Blue Birds Come Today," it seemed both ridiculous and delightful that it had taken me so many years, so much research, so much thinking to write that story.

You are the series editor of the annual *PEN/O. Henry Prize Stories*. How many short stories do you read in a given year, do you think? How do you narrow down your selection?

The exact number is unknown. My graduate assistants and I read about two hundred journals a year, most of them quarterlies containing sometimes as many as six stories each. Throughout the year I make two piles, "No" and "Maybe," and from time to time re-read the Maybes, then reread them again at the end of the reading period to see what's stuck with me and what I think of the story at the moment. The pile of Maybes grows smaller until I'm usually at twenty-five or twenty-six, and then the process begins of picking twenty winning stories and up to five or so recommended stories. Especially at that point, I take my time and think about the strengths and failings of the individual stories. I don't try to make a balanced collection, though it works out that way each time. It's not my mission to give a survey of the year's themes or types of stories being published. The stories I choose for each *PEN/O. Henry Prize Stories* are those that I believe will last.